JADED
EXPECTATIONS

Brickhouse

DEDICATION

To Shondale "GSko" Gregory

You will forever be missed by all of those who loved you. We will always keep Kisha and your family in our prayers.

Something Unexpected.

Published by Phoenix Publishing House, LLC.

ISBN-13: 978-1-955235-01-3

Published by:

PHOENIX PUBLISHING HOUSE
P.O. Box 154855
Lufkin, TX 75904

About The Author

Life is already the hardest it can be, so Brickhouse loves to escape into the fictional worlds she creates. With new books always in the making, she invites her readers to join her in her escape. Her passion for writing dates back to her childhood when she would copy her favorite books word for word and staple the pages together.

Although her greatest inspiration stems from her ability to create worlds where she can be in total control, she will always fondly remember her 7th-grade teacher's inspirational words: *'you have a way with words, and one day it will make you famous'*.

Brickhouse is excited to embark on this journey of writing with readers around the world.

She currently lives in Lufkin, Texas, with her family. She is the owner of Phoenix Publishing House and Phoenix Notary Services.

Feel free to connect with her via:

Instagram: @author_brickhouse

Facebook: Author Brickhouse

SYNOPSIS

Have you felt so unlovable and out of sorts that when authentic love showed up, it appeared too good to be true?

Zora first felt rejection, danger, and pain from her mother at the tender age of five. Despite bouncing from foster home to foster home, she was always determined to get her footing even though she was never quite sure how. The last thing on her mind is love when she finally gets out of her toxic relationship with Sobray…until Rohan.

Rohan is the epitome of the black alpha male with an old school Renaissance man vibe that any woman would be allured by. Being doted on by his mother and four older sisters has entwined an attentiveness every woman craves. His close relationship with his father has provided him with a firm foundation and integrity. He adores his close-knit family but he, as of late, has felt smothered. So much so that he's reluctant to commit to a woman even though he's ready to love. He longs for what his parents have but is he prepared to have yet another person invading his space?

How will Zora respond when Rohan starts to break through her walls? How will Rohan reciprocate if Zora is just another woman in his life trying to play him? They both want love, but can they get out of their own way to see it in each other?

Sometimes something unexpected can be just what you needed.

From Zora's red notebook.

Love Where Are You?

No matter how fast or far I run, I can never catch you.

I'm consumed by the deepest oceans and left with blistered feet for searching for you in the hottest deserts.

Just when I think I've found you, somehow you slip from my grasp, and I'm left standing alone.

Waiting.

ZORA

"Why in the hell are you going through my phone, Zo?"

Sobray marched across the cement floor that contained mildewed cracks that snaked within the foundation. His Samsung Galaxy made a ting sound when it connected with the rusted floor drain. His eyebrows were clenched together, forming a hairy M in the middle of his forehead that glistened with beads of sweat.

"Because the partial message on the screen said something about you dropping dick off tonight! Is that what you were doing last night when I was blowing your phone up? Instead of moving us out of this musty basement, you out here spreading that community peen to anyone that will take it!"

"Nah, you just mad you ain't been getting it. You keep acting like that; you'll be lucky if I let you taste it. It ain't my fault you let yourself go. Walking around here with that big afro and no makeup."

"Well, excuse me for being comfortable in my own skin!"

"Ever since you had that miscarriage, you just let yourself go! God let that baby die because he knew you were weak! You ain't never been able to stand on your own."

My bottom lip quivered from his harsh words. I laid on this air mattress for four days, soaked in my blood. I knew my baby was dead and couldn't bring myself to face the truth.

Ms. Cynthia, Sobray's mother, had to usher me upstairs so that I could bathe and finally go to the hospital.

"You keep on, and you're going to lose me, Sobray. That's my word."

"You ain't going nowhere. Ain't nobody else gone cankle bang and fupa scoop to access that cat. You lucky a real nigga like me even rocking with you," his words stung like Nair coming in contact with my clit.

"It's some good cat under this gut, you bum nigga!"

He threw on his white tee and jogged up the wooden steps that led into the light upstairs. He was unbothered by the fact that once again, he was breaking my heart.

The dark, damp basement reflected how I felt with Sobray. I was no stranger to the ache in the back of my throat as dread slithered up from the rolling in the pit of my stomach.

He was stressing me out, but I could never bring myself to leave him and stay gone. I latched on to him because he was the first person to show me love.

I was seventeen and had just run away from one of many foster homes I had been raised in when I met him.

I hung out on the block with the guys. When the block got hot, they let me make little drops for them here and there, but nothing major. They didn't want me in that life.

They knew I was different because I always had a book in my hand. It was how I met Sobray.

We all started hanging out at his mom's house.

I normally didn't eat out of everybody's plate because some people don't scrub their dishes. However, being homeless humbled me.

"You the only one in the trap with a book," he pried it from my fingertips and read over the synopsis in the back.

"Give me my book back, bro!"

"You a feisty one, huh?"

"Get the hell on for real before I light you up."

"You ain't gone do nothing," he laughed.

"Try me."

"Girl, cut that out and come ride with me somewhere right quick."

"I ain't getting in that hot car with you. Every crackhead rental you have ends up in a high-speed chase. I'm good."

"Scary."

Sobray had a bad attitude, but his swag offset it at times. His almond-shaped wheat-colored face adorned a thick beard. I learned later that those deep-set dark brown eyes were a shadow of his ill-lit heart.

His Cupid's bow lip hid the gap between his teeth that contributed to his lisp. None of which kept him from spewing poison when he got upset.

I didn't have anywhere to stay back then, so I was always in the trap house. It was beyond me why they kept porn on the T.V. twenty-four seven.

They had no shame even though Sobray's mother was there. Cocaine was her drug of choice, and Sobray provided his mother with as much as she wanted.

He felt that if he gave it to her, he could make sure she doesn't get a hold of a bad batch.

We bonded over the fact that both of our mothers were addicts.

I hadn't seen my mother since I was five but being around Ms. Cynthia reminded me of her.

Despite her being an addict, she still kept the house clean and made sure we all ate.

I've only been with one man, and that was Sobray.

It happened one night we all decided to throw a kickback. The house was packed wall to wall.

There was a dice game in the kitchen that we all knew would eventually end in a fight.

The haze from the Blacks and weed in rotation made my hand barely visible in front of my face.

"Come here for a sec," Sobray pulled me to the side and escorted me to the bathroom.

A situationship was developing, but we had yet to make it official.

"Hey, get out the bathroom," he yelled, banging on the locked door.

"My bad, bruh," some sweaty drunk surfaced from the bathroom, offering his apologies to Sobray.

Sobray had a bad attitude, so people did their best to stay on his good side.

"Why are we in the bathroom?"

Sobray didn't respond with his words but his mouth instead.

His soft lips yielded strong kisses that made my body tingle, mostly between my legs.

I was always reading, so I never paid attention to the unhealthy amount of porn that was always played on the big screen.

I had no idea what to do or even if I was ready to do it.

"Sobray…I…don't think I'm ready for this."

"You good ma. I got you," he continued with his kisses as he unbuttoned my jeans. They fell to my ankles, and I instinctively stepped out of them.

I couldn't afford to buy myself underwear, so I would just take a new pair of Sobray's boxers and put them on.

He didn't complain about it because he knew my situation.

He planted kisses all over my full waist kneeling in front of me. Once he was faced with my nakedness, he started to nibble on the button between my legs.

I've never felt anything more pleasurable in my life. I couldn't believe I'd gone this long without experiencing something so cosmic.

"How is that going to fit in me?" I grabbed him by the waist to stop him from proceeding.

"Your body can do unimaginable things, and I'm going to show you every one of them," was the last thing he said before entering me.

"Ouch!"

"Just hold on it's going to stop hurting in a minute," he continued to slide himself inside of me.

His rhythm echoed the beat from Black Youngta's *Hip Hopper* blasting through the speakers.

I couldn't believe my first time was in a bathroom surrounded by a bunch of drunks and drug dealers.

Ever since that night, we've been inseparable. I no longer hesitated about jumping in the car with him or holding his gun along with mine.

Sobray was only a lower-level dealer making a small come up on selling Serenity to college kids. Synthetic weed was the drug of choice at the moment for these kids.

Sobray shelled out wads of cash to me to keep me in the newest kicks and Champion gear. It was my favorite brand to wear. I had every color in various styles.

Now I was sitting down here wondering how I lost myself in him. We're nearly thirty and still living in his mama's basement.

I was pulled from my depressive stroll down memory lane by the murmur of voices and footsteps overhead.

Pop!

Pop!

Pop!

I grabbed my gun and hid behind one of the wall panels I had carved out.

As grimy as Sobray was, I had to be prepared for anything. On the many recent occasions, he's left me alone down here; I would read and ponder my life.

I developed the hiding spot because I knew he wouldn't bat an eye if I died down here.

I secured the panel and waited to see if anyone came down the stairs looking for Sobray.

I watched three guys I've never seen before rummage through our belongings.

Whoever it was knew exactly where Sobray kept his stash of money and Serenity. Sobray was friendly and talked way too much to be a drug dealer.

I've told him on several occasions that those men were not his friend, but you couldn't tell him anything. Sobray felt he had all the answers.

They bagged everything up and left as quickly as they had come.

Once I heard the door slam, I emerged from my hiding spot.

Click Clack.

I cocked my gun just in case someone was lingering behind.

I peeked through the crack in the door, and from what I could tell. The coast was clear.

My muscles became stiff and rigid as my heartbeat started to race.

The house was empty except for Rocko, Isis, and Caesar. The intruders had shot and killed all Sobray's Pitbulls.

Their dark blood had started to soak through the dirty brown worn carpet beneath them.

"What happened, Zo?" Sobray barged in, brandishing his pistol.

"You were robbed. I was hiding downstairs, and three guys came and took everything. I heard the gunshots when they killed the dogs."

Sobray grabbed his head, still holding his pistol.

He kneeled to cradle Rocko. He had him since he was fifteen. He treated that dog as if he was a human being.

Tears formed on his eyelids as he rubbed the heel of his hand against his chest.

"So, you just hid while they took everything and killed my damn dogs? You ain't worth the skin you wrapped in! Get out of my house and don't look back!"

"It's almost midnight, and it's raining!"

"You telling me like I'm supposed to care!"

"Sobray I-"

"Get out!!" He yelled, securing the pistol in the center of my forehead.

I was scared to breathe in fear of him pulling the trigger and ending my life.

"O…okay."

Once he lowered the gun, I ran out of the house without bothering to look back. I only had the clothes on my body and my cell phone tucked in my bra.

I wanted to be free of Sobray now, but I didn't think it would be like this.

I held my arms tightly across my chest as I made my way down the deserted street.

There wasn't much action around this time in Madison, but I still feared for my life.

The hour of walking felt like an eternity in the freezing rain. My hard nipples protruded my shirt as if they wanted to escape the hell I was in too.

I finally made my way to St. Mary's Hospital, where I took a seat in the waiting room. There were a few people, but it wasn't to pack.

I found a seat in the corner as I tried to figure out how I would survive without Sobray.

ZORA

Six months ago, you couldn't tell me that I would be standing on my own. I was able to get into a women's shelter the morning after I left the emergency room.

They had a program that helped me get a job and save money. I finally had enough saved to get my place to stay.

You gotta be kidding me! I rotated the mint condition of Maya Angelou's *I Know Why the Caged Bird Sings* in my hands. I was in complete awe. The hardships of her life resonated with the turmoil in mine. It also reminded me of Sobray, who only reached out for sex these days. Since he was the only man to get this Capri Sun, I relented every time he called.

It wasn't the first turmoil that bonded me with the book, though; it was the memory of when it was first introduced into my life by my mother.

It was my fifth birthday, and although initially, I couldn't pronounce some of the words, I quickly learned them. My mother couldn't afford wrapping paper, so she used a brown paper bag with red string.

She made me my favorite caramel cake. She was an excellent baker. She stuck five candles she dug from the drawer into the finished mouthwatering delicacy.

I blew out the candles and tore open the only gift my mother could afford me at the time.

I didn't care. I knew we didn't have much, even at that age, but I knew she was doing her best.

I left the replacement copy of my book behind at Sobray's, and out of spite, he refused to give it back to me. I was reading it the day we met, so he knew what it meant. It was his way of punishing me for what happened that day. The original copy from my mom was lost in foster care.

The book was the only consistent thing in my life as I traveled from one place to the next growing up. My last foster father got too handsy, and I knew it was time for me to go. Leaving in the middle of the night while the entire house slept forced me to grab what I could and make a run for it. I was almost seventeen at the time, so I doubt if they would look for me shortly after I found myself in Sobray's arms.

I've been searching for a copy since Sobray put me out, but my money was used these days to survive.

I've spent the last six months working doubles and saving every penny to secure my place. A place I could call home. If you've never been in foster care, you wouldn't understand the weight something so simple holds. I made sure I applied steady pressure to avoid ever having a man take anything else from me.

I struggled to fit my hand in the front pocket of my tight jeans. They weren't tight by choice; I just couldn't afford to buy jeans my size.

The stress of being back in homeless shelters and living without Sobray caused me to lose so much weight I didn't recognize myself.

The pants I wore for work today were not only tight, but they were too short for my five-eight stature. I cut off the hem to make them look like capris and tethered the ends.

Moving was my priority, so I made what I had work. I didn't waste money on frivolous things.

The desire for the back had me at war within me. I went back and forth by focusing on the big picture and living my best life.

I counted out three fives and a few ones, nowhere near the amount needed to survive the week. I had to calculate my bus card cost, which was mandatory if I planned on making it back and forth for work. It was too far to walk, or I would.

As I held the book, I could see myself curled up on the couch, reading it with an amazing cup of lavender tea.

I looked down at my backpack as I pondered, stuffing the book inside.

"Can I help you with something?"

I was startled by the owner Rohan approaching me. I came in here often enough to learn his name but never bold enough to hold a conversation. I'm not what you would call a people person.

I feel there is no need to get attached to anyone because people always leave you or alienate you when you no longer served a purpose to them.

"Umm, no, I'm fine," I gave a nervous smile.

"Well, if you do, just let me know. That's one of my favorites too. When I came across it at a book fair, I had to purchase it and add it to my catalog. It's nice to see someone else can appreciate good literature as well," he smiled from ear to ear.

Rohan was six-four in height and built like a linebacker. He looked fairly young, but his salt and pepper hair was so misleading I could never quite pinpoint his age.

His chestnut eyes were solid yet kind. His smile was as white as the ivory from an elephant roaming in Africa. It betrayed something his baritone voice masked…sensitivity.

Once he'd disappeared into the back of the store, I put the book back and left.

There was so point in torturing myself any longer. If I'd stayed, I would've stolen the book.

I gave a glance back over my right shoulder and dashed toward the bus stop. I couldn't be late for work today

Today was the day I got my apartment. The last thing I needed was to lose this Lil' job.

I could still feel the pages of the book on my fingertips as I rubbed them together.

It won't always be like this. I reminded myself. If I wasn't anything else, I was resilient.

I looked down at my Cricket phone at pressed ignore. There was also a message from Sobray wanting to hook up later. I struggled not to respond. I know if I didn't, he would just pop up.

"Isn't this your stop?" The bus driver asked me, forcing me to pull my eyes from the phone.

"Yes, thank you!" I hopped off the bus and crossed the street to head into the call center.

I really wasn't in the mood for people's crap today. Going from the fast money being handed to me from Sobray to a nine to five was not the play.

I made my way to my cubicle, where Sherica was next to me, already logged in.

"Girl, I'm not for these people shit today over these cheap phone plans," she complained.

"Me either. I was thinking the same thing on the bus."

"I told you I would give you a ride to work. You don't have to take the bus."

"I'm fine with riding the bus," I said.

"If you change your mind, just let me know."

"I will," I smiled.

She seemed nice. We were in training together and ended up on the same team on the floor.

I just didn't make it a habit of making new friends. People were unpredictable and finicky, and I didn't need either in my life.

Jilly and I have been friends, well, more like sisters, since her mom was one of my foster parents. CPS felt her mom had too many kids, so they took me to another home against her will.

We had connected while I was in the shelter over Facebook. She insisted I come live with her, but I declined. I needed to learn to stand on my own two feet.

She was the only friend I needed in my life, and her support was enough.

Our lives were the epitome of the difference between having a loving home and being forced to survive on your own.

Jilly was a married mother of two who enjoyed being a stay-at-home wife.

She took pride in caring for her family, and she never got caught up in those women empowerment movements that claimed to uplift women but down others who found solace in caring for their families full-time.

Her locs were always neat, and I was still amazed she found time for the upkeep while running after two toddlers.

She and her husband wanted to have the children close to growing up together and always have each other in school.

They never wanted them to feel alone, and I admired that.

I often wondered why God never designed my mother with the same characteristic.

We didn't spend a lot of time together, but we spent enough. I was a loner anyway, so it never bothered me. Just knowing I had her was enough.

"Good morning Queens!" Lily, a short Latina girl who was on our team, took her seat.

She was always so positive, upbeat, and sincere.

She always had a smile, and her make-up was flawless.

I wished at times I had the nerve to ask her to teach me, but I hated feeling vulnerable.

I sighed as I heard the beeping in my right ear, letting me know that I had an incoming call.

"Thank you for calling Cricket. This is Zora. My operated I.D. is 03461. How may I help you?"

My mind drifted as the ratchet woman complained in my ear.

"I mean, I just paid a $200 bill, and I have another one this month!"

"Ma'am, your payment arrangement does not negate current charges. You have four lines on your account with the Hotspot option. You could cut some of the lines and go to a single line and remove it to save money," I politely suggested.

"I'm not cutting my kid's phones off! They need their damn phones. I want to speak to your supervisor!"

"Ma'am, she's just going to explain the same thing," I told her.

"I don't give a damn. Put her on the phone to say the same thing then!"

"One moment, please."

I pressed the other line on my phone and let it ring, "Yeah, I have a Sup call."

"It's too early, Zora. Did you try to deescalate the call?"

"Yes."

"Okay, put her through."

I didn't even bother doing a warm transfer; I just sent her over to my supervisor.

She never wanted to do anything. I mean, you were asking for the position but never wanted to do the work.

I left myself on unavailable, so I wouldn't get any calls while I finally responded to Sobray's text.

"Nah, I'm good," was my response.

I was tired of being his cum rag. It was time I stop feeling obligated to do whatever he wanted because he helped me when I was on my ass.

I was laughing, listening to Sherica as I waited for his response. He never did.

"Ma'am, you only have 500 megabytes of data. That's not a lot. You spend about thirty minutes on Facebook, and that's gone. You can't expect to stream Netflix all weekend," she rolled her eyes and pressed the mute button. "These cheap ass people get on my damn nerves. All this whining and she on the lowest plan we offer."

I shook my head in agreement.

Eighty calls later, I was on my way out the door.

"Girl, get in this car!" Sherica yelled from her car window.

I rolled my eyes and jumped in the car.

"You can drop me off here," I told her when we were near the bank.

The cold air pricked my skin as I stood in line at the bank, waiting for my turn.

I've never had a bank account before, but Jilly had pressured me to get one if I wanted to be a 'real adult' as she put it.

She's just what I needed in my life. Jilly had it all together. I was hoping she could help figure out a way to get on track.

I could hardly hold my excitement as I got ready to withdraw the money for my deposit and first month's rent.

It was all I had in my account, but I had accomplished the first of many goals I set for myself. I tried asking Sobray for help, but he refused.

"I ain't got shit for you ma'. I'm still trying to recoup from being robbed," was his exact response to my request.

I slid the clerk my withdrawal slip and waited for him to verify my account and give me my funds.

"Alright, Ms. Mitchell, you are all set," he smiled, handing me the white envelope filled with my new future.

I stuffed the money in my bag and made my exit. I had to meet my new landlord in forty-five minutes to sign my lease and get my keys.

"Zora?"

A lady who I didn't visually recognize strangely had an emotional familiarity.

Her hair had a side part with extremely damaged ends, and her course hair refused to lay in the direction she tried to comb it.

"Do I know you?" My face twisted in curiosity.

"I'm your mama. You don't remember me?"

"I'm sure you're mistaken. I haven't seen my mother since I was five."

"Yes, when I lost custody of you. CPS took you from me when your school called. You pulled a pot of boiling water off the stove and got third-degree burns on your arms. It's how you got that scar," she pointed to my left forearm.

I instinctively grabbed my arm, trying to cover my scar. Despite my skin graft, the texture of my arm was still rigid. When I stretched out my arm, it resembled the Appalachian Mountains on one of those old globes in school.

"I remember the incident different. My mother was high and passed out. She left a pot of water boiling on the stove, and I tried to move it before she burned us alive," I snapped. "She didn't even take me to the hospital when I tried to wake her from her high. She told me to rub some butter on it and put a cold towel on it. I was in agony all night. When I got to school, they called the ambulance. They wondered how I even made it through the night, let alone made it to school on time."

"I'm sorry, Pooty-"

"Don't call me that!" Tears formed on my eyelids.

My mother was the only one to call me that growing up. I couldn't believe that I had come face to face with her.

"Zora, I know I wasn't much of a mother to you growing up. As a child, I knew you required more because you are more than I could ever imagine. You've always been smarter, stronger, and more responsible, even at that age. Believe it or not, I poured into you all that I had. It was nowhere near what you needed to fulfill you, but it was all that I had to give. It's no excuse, but I was never taught to be a woman or mother," her eyes pleaded with me to understand.

I didn't. If I were blessed enough to become a mother, my child would never feel alone or unprotected.

She wasn't lying, though. My grandmother was mean and surly. My mother rarely brought me around her because she was ironically afraid that she would hurt me.

My mom was an addict, but she never brought strangers home, rare for someone with an addiction. The polar opposite of Ms. Cynthia, who kept a house full of people. She would rather leave me home alone than leave me with a family member.

"Is it too much to ask for your number?"

I rattled the number off quickly, hoping she wouldn't save it correctly in her phone.

Ever since that day, she'd been calling me, trying to force a relationship I no longer needed or desired.

When I needed a mother, she wasn't there. Equipped or not, it was our job to figure it out together! I don't need one now because the world has already had its way with me.

If she would've loved me properly, I could see Sobray for what he was a long time ago. A narcissist.

Once I arrived at the apartment building, my landlord was waiting.

"That will be one-thousand fifty dollars which include your security deposit."

"Here you are."

I felt as if I was floating as I watched her fill out my receipt. I could feel a huge burden being lifted from me.

"Well, if you need anything, please call me."

"Thank you. I will."

I rolled on the floor of the beige carpet like a wet dog trying to dry off. I couldn't believe I had my place.

I walked around the small one-bedroom, taking it all in.

Bumping into my mom still had me feeling some way. I pushed it out of my mind and headed out. I need to pick up my things from the shelter.

My Uber would be pulling up any minute, and I couldn't wait.

Once I grabbed my things, I headed straight back home. I couldn't wait to unpack and settle in.

*　　　*　　　*

The next morning, I decided to stop by the bookstore again. Seeing my mother had triggered something inside me, and I just needed to get my hands on that book.

"You're back, huh?" Rohan smiled as I walked past him.

I returned a half-smile and went to the section where I initially found the Maya Angelou book copy.

It was still there.

"What are you doing?" Rohan yelled when he walked by and noticed me stuffing the book in my bag.

I bolted out of the store with him on my heels.

My heart was pounding, and I could feel the beads of sweat forming on my forehead.

He gave up the chase after a few blocks, and I ducked into an alley to catch my breath.

I can't believe I just did that! What in the hell is wrong with me?

I can't afford to go to jail. Again.

I've been before for shoplifting. I was just trying to survive at the time. It wasn't something I practiced and another reason I worked so hard. I wasn't giving them a reason to lock me up again. When I was with Sobray, I was willing to be bury under the prison for him in some sick feeling of what I thought was love.

When I made it home, I pulled the book out of my bag. It didn't feel as I thought it would. I knew it was because I stole it from a black business owner who was probably barely thriving.

I've been there enough to notice there haven't been any updates to the store. His catalog was rare but limited. He took so much pride in that store, and I stole from him.

I felt horrible. What have I done?

I sat the book on my bookshelf. It was the only book I had at the time, but I was working on building it. I wasn't going to do that by stealing either.

BAM!

BAM!

BAM!

BAM!

It sounded as if someone was beating on my door with a damn oozy.

"Open the door and stop playing with me!" Sobray yelled. "You think you gone text me your address then tell me I can't come over? I own you!"

"Get off my doorstep before I call the cops on your ass!"

"I wish you would! I will burn this down with you in it! Now open the fuckin' door!"

My hands trembled as I placed my hand on the doorknob. I was stupid for texting him my address.

Kssshhh!

The framed picture of a woman molding a pottery vase with a caption that read *"Mold me Lord"* shattered when Sobray choked me against the wall.

I could feel my trachea swelling under his death grip.

"You think somebody playing with yo' ass girl? I will kill you where you stand!"

He then grabbed a handful of my hair and slung me across the floor.

"Get the fuck off me, Sobray! Get out of my house!"

I clambered across the floor, trying to make it to my gun, but he pulled me back to him by my ankle.

"Uugghh!" I screamed when he kicked me in my side, knocking the wind from me.

"Put your hands up now!" The cop yelled, pointing his Glock at the back of Sobray's head.

One of my neighbors must've called them, and I prayed they didn't report me to the landlord.

"You called the cops? I'm going to kill you bitch when they let me out!"

"Well, that won't be soon. Are you actually stupid enough to threaten her in front of a cop? Bring your ass on!" He roughly pushed him out the door.

The other cop with him stayed behind.

"Ms. Mitchell, this is the information for domestic violence assistance. Take this to the courthouse and get a restraining order in place. I'm not sure if he will get any time or if they will just put a domestic violence hold on him. If they just put a hold on him, then he will be out in four eyes. You need to protect yourself."

I shook my head in understanding and took the paper.

Inside I knew I could never be a part of taking Sobray's freedom from him no matter what he did to me.

Once I had my apartment back to myself, I sat in the middle of the floor and cried myself to sleep. I hated how Sobray and I had become enemies.

He was mean, but at the same time, he was the only one to look out for me when I needed it most.

ZORA

It has been the longest week of my life, and I was glad that it was finally over. Sobray had been calling me nonstop from the county. After the free phone calls, I didn't have money to add to keep talking to him. He apologized over and over and tried to convince me he was a changed man.

He mostly wanted to make sure I wouldn't cooperate with the police so he wouldn't get much time. I wasn't pressing charges, but I was done with Sobray. I think.

This was my first weekend off in a long time. I was exhausted from taking the long route to and from work to avoid Rohan.

I had to wake up early and got home late. Outside of that, the guilt was eating me alive. Despite the hard life I was dealt with, I never took my hardships out on anyone else. I've never felt like the world owed me anything.

The one person who owed me was my mother, and she was too self-absorbed to think of a child she pushed out and abandoned.

I'm not sure if I have other siblings, and up until seeing my mother recently, the thought never crossed my mind.

I pray she didn't damage any other kids as she did me.

I was barely a functional adult in society. Thievery and accepting abuse weren't beneath me.

"Who is it?" I was glad the knock on my door pulled my attention from the stolen literature on my shelf that I couldn't stop staring at.

"Girl, who else knows where you stay? You know I'm your only friend," Jilly laughed on the other side of the door.

"Jillian Adams, if you don't get your butt in here," I pulled her in with a hug.

I was glad to see my friend. She was glowing like melanin sunshine.

"Look at you all grown up! Girl, you have your place! This is huge for you, baby!"

Tears flowed from both of our eyes as the reality of what I had really achieved sank in.

I've never had my own roots, even with being twenty-six years old.

"What happened to your neck, Z?"

"It's nothing," I lied.

"It looks like a handprint. You know how hard someone had to choke you to leave their print bruised on your skin?" She fussed.

"It was just a misunderstanding between Sobray and me."

"I told you to leave that thug alone, Z! You deserve better than him! He keeps showing you who he is. Why do you refuse to believe him?" Her nostrils flared with anger.

"I do now. Trust me. So, catch me up," I said, facing her as I folded into Indian Style on the couch, attempting to break the tension between us.

"First, we pour the wine," she unenthusiastically shoved a chilled bottle in my face.

"Girl, you and this wine mess," I laughed.

I fumbled around in the kitchen. I only had a few dishes, and the only reason I had wine glasses was that I thought they were cute when I was at the Dollar Tree.

I was glad her bottle was a twisting top because I didn't have a corkscrew. I made a mental note to pick up one from the store.

"I'm going to transform you into a cultured lady sooner rather than later, Zora Mitchell. I'm going to show you how to love yourself," she grabbed her glass from the table and marched off.

"Okay, you have your wine now, spill it!" I laughed.

My laughs were genuine with Jilly. I didn't have to put up any walls to barricade myself from her.

I've exposed her to the worst parts of me, and she has chosen to stick by my side.

She has already started to teach me to be kind to myself just by being her.

"Well…."

"Well, what?!" I tossed one hand in the air as if I was serving drinks.

"Elliot is having an affair."

"Shut the front door! Jilly, I know you lying. That man is crazy about you and those bean head kids!"

I couldn't believe what she was revealing to me.

I never saw this coming. They were so happy. There must be more to this!

"No, I'm lying," she fell back on the couch, careful not to spill her wine. "Girl, we along with our bean head kids," she slapped my knee, "is doing just fine. When are you finally going to give me a niece or nephew?"

"As soon as they start being issued with mutual funds," I laughed. "Sobray has me traumatized when it comes to men. I'm cool with being alone. Maybe I'll just become a crazy cat lady."

"A part of your healing is found in the one you choose to share your life with. You must be open to love. You are worthy of love and to be loved. Z, you read like a maniac. You drench of knowledge and strength. Don't let Sobray take the possibility of being loved by a real man from you. Promise me this year you will try to love again."

"Try to what? Get me heartbroken. I'm good on that. Besides, I'm just getting on my feet, Jilly. I want more than to be someone's wife and moth-"

I couldn't finish the word once I thought about what I had just said. How I made Jilly feel."

"I didn't know my life was so low on the totem pole Z. Look, it may not be much to you, but I'm happy being what they need—nurturing and being there when my kids and husband have a bad day. I'm home praying and worshipping. I set the atmosphere of peace and love for them when they return from a cruel world that makes them feel as if they are less than. I won't apologize, and this is my last time dignifying it," her voice quivered as she spoke.

"Jilly, you know I didn't mean it like that. I was just trying to say I want to see what I can achieve. I wish I were that aware if I wanted to be a wife and mother. I'm still figuring it out, and I'm almost thirty! Hell, I'm still getting tossed across the floor by a man that it kills me to fall out of love with."

She smiled, but I could tell her feelings were still hurt.

I was glad she didn't leave. I don't watch television, so it was nice to have a meaningful conversation with my friend.

"So, this should put you right back on your high horse," I teased her.

She smiled, "What did you do?"

I walked over to my empty bookshelf and grabbed the book. My guilt made it seem heavier than it was.

"Z! He gave it back to you! You love this book! I remember you cried for days because he wouldn't give you back this book," she embraced me.

Jilly was a hugger. She was touchy-feely no matter how much I hated it.

She would always say I need more hugs to make up for the ones I missed out on growing up.

"I don't get it. What's the problem?"

"I stole it," I sighed with embarrassment.

"Zora Mitchell, you did what?" She scolded me.

I hated when she used my full name. It was her way of letting me know how serious she was.

I valued her opinion and what she thought of me.

"I know. I know. I just wanted it so bad. I needed it. You know how attached I am to this book.

It's been the one constant thing in my life. It's like a security blanket for me.

"Zora, you're not in those foster homes anymore or being demeaned by some man-child. You have your own home now that you work hard to get. Are you willing to throw that all away to hold on to something from the past? You are not that scared little girl anymore, Z."

"That's the thing. I am still that scared little girl. Jilly, I'm terrified that this will all fall apart. What if I lose my job and can't find another one in time to pay my bills? Or I pay bills but can't get a bus card or eat? I'm barely pulling this off. I've never done this before Jilly," I fought to hold back the tears that ignored my need to be stubborn.

"You're not alone. You know I got your back for whatever through whatever. We ain't switched up on each other, and we're not about to start now. Could you sit down, let me show you something? Grab an extra notebook that you're not using."

I did as she asked. I wrote poetry all the time. I wasn't much of a talker, but I love to express myself through my writing.

"Do you have a black marker and some envelopes? She asked.

"Jilly, why are you sending me on this treasure hunt? What else do you need, girl?" I laughed.

"I think this is it," she smiled from ear to ear like a Cheshire cat. "Do you know how to create a budget?"

"I have a general idea," I snickered nervously.

I was amazing at English, Comprehension, Science, and History. Math and I only got along on payday.

"Come closer. Not trying to be all up on your business or nothing, but how much do you bring home every two weeks?"

"With overtime, which is what all these checks have been, comes to about $800."

"Don't budget off of your overtime. If they stop it, you will get in a bind. Without the overtime, what are we looking at?"

"About $600," I lowered my head.

"What are you embarrassed for? Girl, you are working to take care of yourself the best way you can. You can always promote, find another job or sell one of these damn notebooks with all these bomb poems in them."

Jilly was always pumping me up. She made me feel I could be a CEO or this sought-after author directing movies and stuff.

I looked at the boxed-up notebooks filled with years of raw emotion.

All my clothes fit in one garbage bag, and the three boxes were all filled with notebooks. That's it. That's all I owned.

The small wood kitchen table was here when I viewed the place, and I asked the owner if I could keep it and the couch.

I sanitized everything and made it my own.

I found some thick fabric on clearance and covered the worn antique couch with it. I went to Goodwill to find matching pillows. Well, not exactly matching.

"Focus Z!"

"I Mmmmm," I lied.

I was zoning out. Math did that to me.

"Look, so your income is $1200. What expenses do you have?"

I rambled them off to her. One thing I didn't believe in was creating unnecessary bills.

"The good thing is you don't have excessive bills. You just have your necessities which are lights, gas, rent, food, transportation, and savings."

"How am I supposed to save?"

"When you work overtime is not money to splurge with. Put that in your savings for emergencies. Keep building on that cushion."

"Okay, what are the envelopes for?"

"I know how you are with money. You did awesome saving for the apartment, so I know you have it in you."

I watched her write each bill's name on an envelope, and one was labeled "For Me."

"What is that one for?"

"You have to pay yourself, Z. No one wants to work and not see any fruits of their labor. Always pay yourself, even if it's only a few bucks. It's yours to do with what you want. Maybe buy a certain book the right way," she smiled.

"Do you have direct deposit?"

"No, but I can get it in place," I eagerly let her know I was all on board for my life, heading in the right stable direction.

"Do that! In the meantime, put money for each bill in its designated envelope. This is your first month, so that it will be a rough estimate. This month you gauge everything other than the rent. You know what that will be every month."

I listened intently, making sure I didn't miss anything.

I was excited. I feel like God is redeeming the time in my life. I'm on my way to greatness.

Jilly and I finished our bottle of wine before leaving to get her kids from school.

"You know you have to take that man his book back, right?" Jilly said, grabbing her purse and heading out as I followed.

"I know. I'm going to try and sneak it back in."

"Scary! Return it like an adult, and maybe he won't have your butt locked up, crazy lady," she laughed hysterically.

"Byeeeee Jilllyy!" I pushed her out the door while she was still laughing.

She was right. I need to fix this. That's my favorite place to hide and read. Most time, I doubt if

Rohan even knew I was there, so I was shocked when he chased me out of the store!

ROHAN

Three Years Ago...

"You wait a week before our wedding to hundreds of people, including our family, to tell me you don't want to get married?" I yelled at Nikia.

"Ro, please don't make this harder than what it is. This wasn't an easy decision to come to."

"Where was this conviction when I was shelling out thousands of dollars? The money I could've used to open my bookstore!"

"Rohan, I need a man with more drive with a little thug in him."

"Nikia, we live in Madison! How much of a thug can you find in this city! Women always say they want a good man, but when you get one, you bounce to chase a no-good Negro that will make your edges fall out."

"Look, I'm not going back and forth with you. I will have my sister pick up the rest of my things."

"Don't bother. I will have them shipped to you. Where will you be?"

"That's none of your concern. Send it to my parents' house."

"Wait a minute! You mean to tell me you are already living with this Negro! Woooow! Get out of my house, Nikia, before I lose it!"

Once she was gone, I grabbed my keys to break the news to my parents.

As I was driving, I noticed an eighteen-wheeler merging onto the Beltway. There was a car next to me so I couldn't get over it.

Maybe he will slow down. I thought.

"What the hell!" I yelled before being sideswiped by the truck.

I spent out of control before going unconscious.

"Baby, are you okay? Can you hear me?" I could vaguely hear my mother's words call to me in the darkness.

"Wake up, baby," she pleaded.

My eyes felt like they were sealed with Gorilla Glue. I wanted desperately to open them, but they wouldn't.

I spent months in the hospital recovering and learning to walk again.

Nikia didn't come to the hospital, not once. My mother told me later she had to keep my sisters from issuing her out a beat down.

That was the day that broke me. I've been putting myself back together physically and emotionally ever since.

I know most men would start to mistreat all women, but I refused to let Nikia change who I am. In the end, it would be her loss.

I took the money from the wedding and opened it in a bookstore.

People thought I was crazy for leaving my job in corporate America to open a bookstore in the black community.

I wasn't crazy; I just decided to live my life the way I wanted while taking risks that I could be proud of one day.

ROHAN

Present Day

I was so disappointed in the beautiful stranger who had visited my store on so many occasions. She didn't know, but I secretly watched her every time she would come in.

The only reason I caught her stealing the book was that I finally dared to ask her out for coffee.

I'm the youngest of three sisters. My parents have been married for over thirty years and are still just as in love as the day they met.

No infidelity, outside children, separations, or raised voices during disagreements. I grew up in a house filled with love and understanding.

I wanted something so beautiful and sustainable like that, but I also fear being suffocated like I've been all my life. I also couldn't weather the devastation of being cheated on again.

When I tell people I'm the youngest, they assume I'm spoiled. I am. My mother and older sisters also smother me.

My sisters run everyone I attempt to date off with their overbearing ways, except for LaDana.

They force her until I can't tell anymore if I like the woman or if they've gotten in my head.

My mom has since backed off because she desperately wants grandkids from me and acts as if I'm on her biological time clock.

I still wondered about the quiet stranger who hid in the corner of my store at times and read for hours on end.

I didn't care that she took the book. I hated to see that side of her. To have my fantasy ruined gutted me like fresh fish.

"Heeeyyy sexy man!" LaDana sang, walking in with my usual cup of coffee.

LaDana was four-eleven and feisty. She wasn't bashful, but she was a bit aggressive for my taste. She was beautiful and consistent with hopes of wearing me down.

"Hello yourself, sexy," I smiled, greeting her.

She handed me my coffee while holding on to my waist with the other hand.

"What you over here doing in this dusty bookstore," she teased.

"Definitely not making any money," I sighed in defeat.

"I told you to turn this joint into a bar or sell it," she said.

"I can't do either. This is my baby, even if it's not producing now. We need black literature in the hood."

"Apparently, we don't because all of these books are starting to look antique with all this dust. You need to clean up," she laughed, nudging me. "When are you taking me out?"

"When you learn that I'm a real man and act accordingly. I like to pursue my women so they know they wanted and desired. They'll never have to question either. I don't need to be led. I understand the importance of leading. Trust the process, love," I smiled at her.

I could tell she was a bit off-put by my response, but she'll be okay.

I'm not one of these men who wanted my woman making the first move. I would never make her feel like she must carry the weight anything while she has me by her side.

My shoulders are wide enough to carry any burden, care, or concern her beautiful mind could fathom.

My chest is broad enough to shield her from anything that would have to tear through me to get to her. I would gladly be shredded for her.

"Well, you know where I'm at, Malcolm X, when you're ready," she smiled half-heartedly as she made her exit.

I sat the coffee on the counter and took her advice, and did some light cleaning.

It was a perfect way to waste time until it was time to meet my parents for dinner.

We are a big family that spends a lot of time together to reinforce our bond as a unit. We love catching up with one another on that one day a week.

I was over at my parents' a bit more often, being a bachelor who hated to eat alone. I could cook my butt off, though, so don't get it twisted.

I couldn't believe what I was seeing. It was the beautiful thief.

I watched her outside the store struggling within to swallow her pride to come in. I had to wipe this huge smile from my face before she came inside.

I was elated that she was exactly the woman I perceived her to be.

The warm breeze from Lake Michigan caused her fro to blow softly.

It reminded me of Foxy Brown from back in the day.

Her skin was flawless, and she only adorned lip gloss that sparkled in the sun.

I watched her exhale harshly and make her way in.

I quickly bolted behind one of the bookshelves out of view.

I wanted to see if she would just slip it back on the shelf or face me and right her wrongs.

"Hello?" She yelled.

I appeared from behind the shelf holding a book as if I was putting it away.

"What are you doing here? Come to steal something else?"

She rolled her eyes as if I were trying her patience.

I wasn't about to make this easy for her. If this would be my last encounter with her, I had to drag it out whatever way I could.

"No," she replied humbly.

"I'm confused! Why are you here?" I raised my voice.

"Who are you yelling at? Look, I know I was wrong but I came to make it right. What you not about to do is disrespect me and talk to me crazy! I made a mistake and I apologize," she pulled the book from her bag and extended it to me.

"I have a right to yell! Why would you steal from a black owned business as if we as a people don't have it hard enough? Then you think you can just apologize and it's all over with? I should put you in jail!"

"What's going on over here?" LaDana barged into the store at the most inopportune time.

"Nothing," I said looking at Zora who was clearly humiliated.

She sat the book on the counter and rushed past LaDana.

As she walked by the glass I could see her wipe away a tear.

I took it too far and didn't mean to embarrass her.

I forget how my deep voice resonates.

If LaDana hadn't interrupted I was going to ease up on her in hopes of breaking the tension.

I was going to tell her to keep the book and offer her a job here.

I couldn't pay her but for just a couple of hours she could take any book she wanted on the days she worked.

I just wanted her around in an attempt to get to know her.

That was all ruined now.

"What's going on?" LaDana clearly wanted an answer about something that wasn't her business.

Therefore I hadn't taken her out since inviting her to our family barbeque. She's too overbearing. Like my sisters!

If I were to bet my last dollar on the reason they vouched for her this would be it.

"Nothing. Shouldn't you be working?' I tried to change the subject.

"She was trying to steal something, huh?" She pursed her lips to one side.

"No Dana. Look, I have to close," I told her.

"I know. I know. It's the day you have family dinner. If you get some cameras these hood chicks wouldn't be able to steal from you," she laughed leaving.

I'm surprised she even had a job. She was always over here pushing up on me so I know she's not working.

I wasn't the type of man to sit around and gossip. What transpired between the stranger and I wasn't Dana's business.

I went over to the counter and picked up the book.

A note fell out with my name on it. How did she know my name?

Rohan,

I know you probably won't believe me but I'm not a thief. I'm a lot of things but that's not one of them. I'm sorry I took the book but it holds a value to me I can't begin to put in this letter. I still had no right to take anything that you work so hard for. Our black business must thrive in order to keep the black dollar in circulation. That can't happen if we take from our own. I'm truly sorry. I wrote this just in case I didn't have the nerve to tell you face to face.

Zora.

So that was her name…Zora. She looked like a Zora with her high cheek bones and golden bronze skin. The thought of her full lips caused the right corner of my mouth to pull into a half smile.

"I'm sorry but I'm closed," I told the man walking into my bookstore.

"This is a legal matter," he responded.

"Legal matter?"

"Yes, your store is going into foreclosure and we have a potential buyer that is interested in the property who can take it off of your hands."

"So let me guess? They send the brother down here to try and talk me out of my business. How can you help them gentrify our neighborhood? They just want to push us out remodel and raise the property value so that our people can no longer afford to live in their own neighborhoods."

"Man save the '*I have a dream*' speech. As you can see, WE don't support US. That's why you here barely keeping your head above water. I came here because the 'powers that be' at the bank would rather just wait for you to lose it and get nothing! I came as a courtesy. Not all of us are sellouts! Some of us have jobs and still look out. Just in other ways," he dropped the paperwork on the counter and walked out.

"Man!" I yelled out in the empty store.

There's no possible way I could dictate in words what it means to me to be a pinnacle of knowledge in my community.

I'm just not ready to let it go but what else can I do?

I walked over and picked the papers up. Just as I suspected, they wanted to put a Starbucks here. It would force the black-owned coffee shop next door out of business due to their mass marketing and recognizable brand.

I shook my head. Not only did I have to figure out something for my own store but I had to look out for the business next door.

Ms. Alice has owned that shop for over fifteen years. She opened it after her husband died.

With the help of her children they have managed to remold and change with the times keeping them in business.

She's too old to run the store now but one of her sons is the general manager.

They're not having the problems that I am because black people actually drink coffee and Ms. Alice's cakes are renowned in the hood.

"That fool trying to buy you out too?" Clayton asked.

Working next door to each other caused us to become close. I didn't believe in frivolous relationships so if I called you friend, I meant it.

"Yep," I said dropping the document back on the counter.

"He came in the shop trying to act like he all for the people. At the end of the day he a snake! I told his ass I ain't selling my mama store she used her blood, sweat and tears to build. Hell, we are doing just fine between the coffee and the cakes. Matter of fact the coffee cakes banging," he joked.

I wasn't in the mood to laugh. I wasn't doing as well.

"I'm glad y'all don't have to worry," I sighed.

"Look man. Every business has growing pains. You've only been here a few years. It takes time to build and establish a clientele," he encouraged me.

"I know man but what was I thinking opening a bookstore in the hood?"

"You were thinking that knowledge is power brother. Ain't no shame in wanting to pour that into your community."

"Right on."

"Keep your head up brother," he extended his hand and embraced me with the other.

"We still on for pool this week?" I asked him.

"Yeah, I'll beat on you some more," he laughed leaving the store.

Clayton's words encouraged me. I need to figure something out.

ROHAN

My stomach hardened with nausea as I approached my store. My windows were busted and the inside of my store vandalized. Gang signs were spray painted on my walls and I came undone.

A painful tightness formed in my throat as I fought to hold back the tears invading my eyes.

I was beyond hurt that people could stomp on my passion with no regard for my sacrifice.

The accident a few years back left me with a noticeable limp. I've been fighting the driver's company in an ongoing lawsuit since. You would think it was a no brainer but they were dragging this out in hopes that I would settle for less than I deserve.

Every month I scraped together the money to pay bills at my house and the bookstore.

No matter how much good I put out into the Universe it just keeps returning me lemons.

Every time I try to take a step forward in this business, I'm being pushed back two.

When will it be my turn to win?

Anguish washed over me and the tears I was warring with took the win.

Contrary to popular belief, black men do feel. We do hurt and we also get discouraged.

My shoulders are broad enough to carry it but lately I've wanted my rib to lean on in times like this.

Her words would be as strong a mother's prayer in the midnight hour for a child who won't let her heart rest. Yet, soothing enough to calm the most vicious storm stirring inside me.

"Is…is…everything okay?" Zora stammered as the broken glass crumbled under her feet.

"Yeah," I said trying to wipe away my tears hoping she wouldn't notice.

"What happened?" She asked.

"I'm not sure. Is there something I can do for you?"

"I was just walking by and saw the mess. I wanted to make sure you were okay."

"I'm okay. Just another reason I should close this place down. No one in this neighborhood wants to read. They have phones and all that other stuff now. I can't afford to keep the doors open anyway."

I grabbed the garbage can and started to clean.

I looked over and noticed Zora sitting her things down.

She grabbed another garbage can and started to help clean.

"You don't have to do that."

"I know but I want to. Some of us in this neighborhood do appreciate this place," she smiled.

I don't think I've ever seen anything so beautiful.

"Thank you," I returned the smile.

"Hey, why don't you start doing poetry slams or open mics? You can ask the store next door if they could donate what doesn't sell at the close of business and we can sell them. Maybe allow it to be B.Y.O.B."

"I don't drink and I don't think alcohol would be a good idea."

"Noooo," she laughed. "Bring your own beverage."

"I think we should clarify it but I love the idea. Maybe we can meet here and discuss it more in detail?"

"I...don't...know, "she replied nervously.

"C'mon, this was your idea. Don't leave me hanging," I opened my arms wide.

"Okay," she relented.

I guess this was one upside to the assault on my store. I got to spend more time getting to know Ms. Zora.

We made small talk as we cleaned the store.

"Your man ain't going to be mad about you hanging out helping me, is he? I would hate to have to beat him up in front of you," I teased.

She laughed, "I'm as single as a dollar bill. Kind of getting out of a bad relationship."

"I can understand that. It took me years to get my fiancé out of my system after we split."

"I hope it doesn't take me that long," she said going back to wiping the walls.

Neither of us pried into each other's past. I guess we both felt it was weird to pour out the stains of your past to a stranger.

Once we restored order, I realize the damage wasn't as bad as I initially thought.

"It looks so much better in here. I can come and help you paint tomorrow if you like. We can talk more about the poetry slam," she smiled.

I was elated.

"You don't have to do that," I told her.

"I want to," she laid her hand on mine and it was as if my heart paused for a moment.

"Okay. I will be here at nine but you can come whenever. Can I give you a ride home?"

"Umm…no thank you," she refused.

"I wouldn't feel right having you walk home now that it's dark outside."

"Okay."

"Great. Let me lock up and get my keys."

I was mesmerized by Zora's entire vibe. She was a bit rough around the edges but she had so much depth to her. She could hold an intelligent conversation. She was so aware about what was going on in our community and world. I could see us on the couch reading our favorite novel with her legs resting in my lap.

"Hey sexy," LaDana sang exiting the coffee shop next door.

It was her night to close but her flattery was unwarranted at this moment.

Zora was already hesitant to deal with me and I don't want her to run off.

Last time LaDana butted in she left the store abruptly.

I mean, we were in heated conversation but none the less I could've smoothed things over if I weren't interrupted.

"Hey Dana," I replied dryly.

"Hey Dana? That's all I get?" She crossed her arms and tapped her foot in irritation.

"That's all you ever get. I'm confused about your actions," I told her.

"Rohan, I'll let you talk to your friend. I can walk home. I will see you tomorrow."

"You will do no such thing. I offered to take you home and that's exactly what I'm going to do."

I hit the button to unlock my car and escorted her in the passenger seat while I set some boundaries with LaDana.

"Okay," she complied and made her way into the car.

"LaDana, we are friends. We chop it up here and there but what you're making it seem like in front her is inappropriate. If you can't respect me the same way I do you then we can't share space."

"I didn't mean any harm. My apologies," she said rubbing my bicep.

I stepped back from her, "Good night Dana."

I rounded my car to join Zora who was clearly uncomfortable with the exchange with Dana.

"Is that one of your groupies?" She asked.

"No just a friend. She works next door so she comes over and chops it up from time to time. We've never dated, kissed or anything like that," I assured her.

"Uuuhhum," she poked her tongue into her cheek and inhaled a long breath. "It's not my business anyway."

"Look, being all tough may be your defense mechanism but you don't have to be like that with me. I don't want anything from you but to get to know you Zora."

"Men always want something eventually. No one does something for nothing," her face tightened.

"I would love the opportunity to prove to you otherwise."

It was as if my heart and stomach were playing kickball as I waited for her to respond.

"You can just let me out at the corner."
She wasn't moved by my declaration. I can't blame her. I'm sure all men said he same thing I just did but their actions showed otherwise.

I hope she knows she's not getting away from me that easily.

"I can take you to your front doorstep Zora. It's no problem at all."

"I don't let strangers know where I live," she shoved her phone in her bag and hopped out of my car like I was a creepy Uber driver she was trying to escape.

I watched until she disappeared out of site. I secretly prayed she would show up tomorrow.

I selected *Two Occasions* by The Deele as my song to vibe to on the way home. I was drawn to Zora. I just wish I could be sure she was feeling me.

LADANA

If Rohan thinks I'm about to let him slip through my fingers he has another thing coming. I've been sweet talking his ass for a year now and some new hood rat from around the way is not about to ruin that for me.

Rohan is everything a man should be. He's considerate, family oriented, handsome, educated, loves God and his mama.

I know he's faithful as well. He told the story of how his fiancé broke off their engagement one week prior to the wedding. He was mortified. That's how our friendship began and why he explained he wasn't going to rush into another relationship.

He said he's not dating anyone unless he could see them in his future. He's not wasting his time otherwise.

Since then we've had this flirtatious banter going on. He's never tried to set boundaries with me prior to today which had me pissed. I've been marinating that dick and I'll be damned if I let another woman come in and take my spot.

I guess it's my fault for not being more upfront about my intentions in the beginning. I just wanted to respect his desire to take his time to find love again.

I personally believe in a man chasing the woman. That love hit different when they had to hunt for you. They value you more because they know the worth attached to you. I mean I joke with him about taking me out to let him know that I want more.

Being the man that he is I know I must handle this situation with a certain delicacy and wit.

Rohan is not the type of man to be manipulated or told what to do. He knows who is and where he's going in life. He's the type of man you can build with not crumble under due to a bunch of childish games spewing from some man-child.

I'm not giving up that easily on you Rohan Jefferson.

I quickly called Esdee to give her the 411.

"What's up girly," she answered weirdly chipper.

This was not her normal persona so I wasn't sure what had gotten into her. I didn't have time to figure it out either.

"Tell me why I was closing the shop and your brother comes out with some girl."

"What girl?" I could tell her interest was piqued.

"The same one who stole a book out of his store a few days ago. I don't like her. Something is off about her."

"Yeah, the fact that she's a thief."

"Well, I flirted with him like I always do on my way out and can you believe he tried to check me in front of her?"

"What?"

"Girl, yes. I didn't know how to respond to it so I just apologized. Well, he dropped her off at home so I just wanted to give you a heads up about your new sister in law," I laughed.

"Chile, please. You know we're not having that riff raff around us. Thanks for the heads up you know I'm on it."

"Alright, talk to you later," I ended the call.

ZORA

"Jilly, I have a code red! I need you to come over!"

"Girl, I'm on my way!"

That was our code when either of us had some tea. It was corny but we always did our own thing.

It only took Jilly twenty minutes to arrive which gave me time to have our wine poured up and ready.

I know I said that I wasn't ready for anyone to come into my life at this time but Rohan was making me feel some type of way. That's not the only thing I needed to talk to Jilly about though. Sobray was out of county and back to texting me again.

It was something about Rohan so serene yet strong. He was everything Sobray wasn't yet I was still drawn to him. Sobray and I had history. A history that kept coming back to bite me in my ass.

I know Sobray is not good for me but something in me weakened when it came to him. At one point we were all each other had.

Rohan was showing me something else though. I was starting to covet the potential of being loved the right way. Witnessing the emotion he felt when his store was vandalized exposed a vulnerability in him that was attractive.

Something about seeing a black man cry touches the soul of a black woman. Not them bullshit cries when they cheat and lie to get you back either like Sobray was currently doing.

Rohan stood for the black men who were doing all they could and to no avail the world just keeps beating them down.

Knock. Knock.

"What's the tea sis?" Jilly laughed as I pulled her inside.

"So, I took you advice and returned the book. It was not the best experience to say the least. He tried to charge me up but I ended up leaving when his lil' girlfriend from next door interrupted us."

"Girl what?"

"Yes, so I still put a note in there to explain about the book just in case such a situation occurred. Well, I was walking by his store today and someone vandalized it. I caught him crying."

"Awwwee," she wiped an imaginary tear.

"I ended up coming inside and helping him clean up. We talked about starting a poetry night or open mic night to help raise money for the store. I'm really geeked about it too. It was all good until ole' girl from next door interrupted again. She was hatin' and I really didn't have time to figure out what they had going on. I allowed him to drop me off at the corner of my street. Before I got out he did explain that nothing ever happened between them."

"The fact that he felt the need to explain himself says a lot Z. So, are you feeling him?" She took a sip of wine.

"I didn't say all of that but I do get to hang out at the bookstore so that's a win in itself," I smiled.

"Are you going to read one of those deep ass poems from those hundreds of notebooks you have stacked in the corner collecting dust?"

"Maybe," I popped my lips. "Yes, I am feeling him though. I think. I don't know."

"Uhhumm," she took another sip. "So, what do you know about him?"

"He's thirty-two. Based on our conversation at the bookstore he's educated, the store is his passion. He was heartbroken that it was destroyed. It made my heart smile to see the hope return to his eyes after we cleaned the place. I'm going by tomorrow to help him paint too."

"Girl, that's how you spending your off day? Painting?" She laughed.

"It's for a good cause and you love how much I love that bookstore."

"Now I see why," she erupted in laughter.

"Whatever," I threw up my hand and rolled my eyes. "Also…Sobray hit me up. He wants to come by and apologize in person."

"You know he's a bald-headed ass lie! He is trying to talk upon some cat! Stay away from him! Your life is heading in the right direction and the last thing you need is his pernicious ass sabotaging you!"

"I know. He just sounds different now."

"Yeah, because his ass been locked up for a couple of months with nothing but time to think of new lies. He just want to see if you're still wrapped around his finger Z."

"You're right."

"I have some news of my own. I'm pregnant. Again," she sighed.

"Why aren't you happy?"

"We can't afford another baby. We're barely making it now."

"I'm sure everything will be fine. Once you look into that baby's eyes it will all be okay," I smiled.

"I'm getting an abortion. My husband doesn't know I'm pregnant yet," she fumbled anxiously with her hands.

"Abortion? Jilly you don't believe in abortion. You can't be serious," I moved closer placing my hand over hers.

"I know but I can't put that stress on Elliot. He doesn't complain or make our family feel like a burden but I notice the subtleties when he's handling the finances for our family."

"Like what?"

"His blood pressure has been up lately. He has to drink while he does it. Stuff like that."

"First of all, his pressure probably high because of all that damn red meat you be frying. Second, that man grown he can drink when he pay them bills. Hell, we all drink paying bills," I laughed. "Why do you think I always have wine up in here now," I lifted my glass causing the wine to swirl into a mini cyclone.

"You're joking but I know my husband," her smile faded.

"Well, you know I got your back no matter what. I'll even go with you if you decide to go through with this. Promise me you will tell Elliot. This is not just your baby, it's his too. He has a right to know."

"This is my body!"

"And that's his seed! Tell him!"

"You don't know what it's like to have a family or husband! Hell, you sitting here thinking about allowing a man who beats the crap out of you back in your life! Who are you to give me advice?"

"Wooowww," I exhaled heavily.

"I'm sorry. I didn't mean that."

"It's my job to ask the hard questions Jilly. I got your back and you would do me the same way. I got your back through whatever and whenever," I embraced her.

The weight of Jilly's decision caused her to break within my arms.

Her back expanded under my hand as she cried frantically.

There was eventually silence between us as I allowed her to feel…to process.

Life is hard. Life is complicated and there is no redo's no matter how many fits we throw. Despite the unfairness that's launched at us we must find our way through the best way we can.

I was praying that Jilly found her way through this and made a decision she could live with.

*   *   *

THE NEXT DAY.   I twirled around in the partially cracked mirror that was also something else left behind from the previous tenant.

I found some cute white capris that wrapped around my butt tighter than a melted Laffy Taffy wrapper.

I immediately regretting the off shoulder yellow top. It was a change from my Champion gear I was used to wearing at one point.

I never showed skin and here I was risking it all for Rohan.

What was I thinking? This is not the type of attire you paint clothes in. I was too cute to change so I would just bring an old shirt to put on over it.

Once I arrive Rohan already had everything ready so we can start painting.

"I wasn't sure you would show up."

"Why is that?"

"Well, after the stunt LaDana pulled I wasn't confidant that you still wanted to help me."

"I offered because I genuinely wanted to. I didn't have any ulterior motives or expectations. I love this bookstore."

"I know. I used to see you hiding in your favorite spot in the dim corner in the back. I added that little lamp on the shelf just for you," he smiled proudly revealing the whitest teeth I've ever seen on a chocolate man.

I had a thing for pretty teeth. It wasn't a sexual attraction; I was just enamored by perfect white teeth. Male of female I would stare.

Jilly would always tease that I should be a dentist due to my obsession.

I often thought of it but I've never really been stable enough to consider school or pursuing a degree.

"Where did your mind just go?" Rohan asked interrupting my wayward thoughts.

"I was just thinking how white your teeth are and that I should go to school to become a dentist," my mouth fell open with utter shock that I shared my naked thoughts so easily with him.

"Thank you and you should. Why haven't you gone back to school," he asked handing the coffee he had waiting for me.

I wanted to tell him I didn't want coffee from that hood rat next door but I decided to be an adult.

I just hoped he watched her fix it.

"It's from the new coffee machine I purchased for our poetry slash open mic night," he said as if he could read my thoughts.

"In that case it's amazing," I snickered. "And to answer your question, I just got some stability in my life. Up until now I had to worry about keeping a roof over my head and food in my stomach."

I had no idea why I was sitting here telling this man all my business. Something about him was easy...unlike my life or Sobray.

There was no judgement in his eyes...only sincerity.

It was as if he was trying to see the real me and let me know that however that person was, it was okay.

I could be wrong but my intuition is never off. My mom thought I had a gift to see because of the things I would warn her about.

"I'm always amazed by black women," his eyes sparkled as the locked with mine.

"What do you mean?"

"Everything meant to break y'all you find a way to make it a foundation to stand on and scream try again world!" He waived his fist triumphantly in the air.

It was corny but it made me laugh.

"Yeah, I guess. We better get to painting. I'm not trying to be stuck with you all day."

"That wouldn't be so bad now would it Ms. Zora," he licked his lips.

My eyes began examining the floor as lust permeated through me.

I can't remember the last time I felt the caress of a man.

"Let's just paint man," I laughed flicking paint his way.

"Oh, so you want a paint fight?" He put his cup down and made his way to the other pan of paint.

"You wouldn't! You can't be playing like that around a black girl with natural hair," I attempted to negotiate.

"Well since you say it like that, I would have to say that I don't want any of that smoke ma'am."

"Alright then let's make some magic," I flashed a smile.

"Woman anybody under two hundred pounds trying to get on this ride requires a waiver. I'm not liable for anything that happens to you. Messing with me you'll end up with a fractured lower back and a puffy twist out," he laughed.

"Well then. Thank you for that information but I just meant magic of bringing this store back to life," I timidly covered my mouth to laugh.

His comment had my nipples hard enough to crack walnuts.

"Well, hello there people," LaDana waltzed in with some pants so tight the seam was eating at the crack of her ass.

"Hey Dana. What's up?" Rohan asked.

"Nothing much. You know I stop by at least once a day to check on ya' big head," she slithered across the wood floor over to Rohan.

"You remember Zora don't you?" He asked her.

"Oh, hey girl. How you been?"

She was so fake but I refused to let her see me sweat. Not that I was. I could see right through that cheap sew-in she was flipping over her shoulder.

"I've been well. Thank you for asking. Rohan, I'm going to step out and make a call. I told you I'm not going to be stuck with you all day so be ready to work when I come back," I told him.

"I'm all over it," he laughed.

I pulled my phone out at soon as I was out of sight to call Jilly.

This girl was like a tick on a dog sucking the life from it. She just refused to let go.

I waited for Jilly to pick up. Checking on her took my mind away from snatching LaDana bald.

"I'm still preggo you don't have to stalk me," Jilly didn't bother giving me a hello because she knew why I was calling.

"I told you I got you no matter what. I just wanted to see how you were doing?"

"I'm good."

"You still haven't told him, have you?"

"No Z. I don't need you pressuring me about this right now."

"Okay love. Do you want to watch the Presidential Debate later?"

"You and your political obsession," she laughed contagiously through the phone causing me to join her.

"It's my guilty pleasure and I make no apologies for it woman."

"How do you know your lil' boo not taking you out after y'all done with the paint date."

"It's not a paint date. I'm just helping him and we're finalizing some plans for our first poetry slam."

"Tell me anything because I'll believe it," she said sarcastically.

"Girl, whatever! I'll keep you posted," I barked before ending the call.

When I turned around a twinge stabbed at my heart.

"Sobray what are you doing here?" I stammered.

"I followed you here since you haven't texted me back. I didn't think it would be a good idea to pop up at your house."

"Why in the hell are you following me? I made it clear when I wrote you that I was done."

"I wanted to give this back to you," he reached in his back pocket and handed me the book.

"I don't want it."

"You love this damn book. Take it. I put a little something inside for you," spittle of saliva showered my face from his lisp.

I slowly reached out and took the book. Inside was an envelope full of money.

"I can't take this."

"You can and you will. I taught you better than that. Never give a nigga back his money woman."

"Is everything okay out here?" Rohan stuck his head out the door interrupting Sobray's finesse.

"Man we good homie," Sobray rudely replied.

"I was asking Zora," he clapped back.

"Nigga I don't give a fuck who you talking to."

"Negro what? I'll break ya' lil' young ass down where you stand!"

"Sobray you need to leave! Now!"

"Girl you have more drama than a lil' bit with yo' thieving ass!"

"Bitch what?" I turned to LaDana nosey ass.

She was always in my business!

Sobray grabbed me before I could light into her ass.

"Rohan I better leave before I end up in jail."
"It looks like both of y'all vacation there often."

"LaDana that's enough you need to get from in front of my store too!" He snapped walking back inside.

"I'll walk you home so you can tell me about this new nigga checkin' for you with his fake ass David Banner lookin' ass," Sobray offered.

"Look stay the hell away from me!" I marched off.

I was livid that Sobray and LaDana had ruined my chanced with Rohan.

LaDana was right about one thing. I did have a lot of drama and I know Rohan wants no pieces of that.

ZORA

"LaDana what the hell are you doing?" I pushed her away from me reinforcing the personal space she violated once again. "That is completely inappropriate! I don't know what has gotten into you but I'm not feeling it at all."

"It was just a peck. Why are you trippin'?"

"Because you've been doing way to much lately. If I want you like that I would make it crystal clear!"

"We always play around like this. What is the big deal? Your lil' friend have you acting real new in here."

"We've never kissed Dana. We flirt here and there and hug but we've never taken it to any other levels. This has nothing to do with Zora it's about you keep throwing yourself at me and I find it unattractive. You need to leave Dana."

"Whatever Ro. I didn't throw myself at you but you are so closed off to love that you are afraid someone is going to break you again! I'm a good woman and I will not apologize for going after what I want. You don't have to put me out because I'm not coming over to this dry ass store anymore anyways!"

"I'm not closed off. I'm just not that into you."

She stomped her mad ass out the store. I followed behind when I noticed that Zora hadn't come back in yet.

Zora said she was single so I'm not sure who the guy was that she was speaking with.

She was also holding a book similar to the one she stole from me.

This neighborhood is sketchy so I thought it would be a good idea to check on her.

I wasn't expecting the dude to lash out. I don't start fights but I put a Negro on his back with no hesitation.

LaDana was already pissed that I had curved her once again so her exchange with Zora didn't have deescalate the situation any.

Zora and I were both being cornered by people we didn't want. I gathered as much when she told him she could get herself home.

That's my girl. I smiled on the inside low-key that she didn't leave with that lowlife.

I looked down at my watch and it was time for me to wrap up what I was doing so I could get home. It was my turn to host family dinner and I was dreading it.

I was over the weekly pressure of me finding a woman from my sisters.

I was a healthy, strong, fiscally responsible and loving black man and I want them to trust the love and support that they've instilled in me.

Arguing with a black woman was like fighting a losing battle. Even if you're right you're still wrong.

As I was leaving I noticed Zora walking down the street she had me drop her off on. I parked far enough away that she couldn't tell I was watching.

She was on her phone waving her hands dramatically. I could imagine she was telling the person on the other end about what went down.

Once she disappeared inside I drove down the street. I caught another tenant coming out of the building and walked inside. I looked on the mailbox and saw Z. Mitchell. That was her and she was in apartment five.

I tapped my phone on my leg trying to decide if I wanted to invade her space or not.

At this point I had nothing to lose. Zora was a flight risk at this point. If the wind blows wrong she's on the move. It was becoming exhausting but from what I know of her so far she was worth it.

I exhaled heavily and knocked on the door waiting for her to answer.

"Who is it?" She yelled from the other side of the door.

"Rohan."

"How do you know where I live?" She demanded.

"I was leaving the store and saw you come inside. I'm not stalking you I just wanted to check on you and make sure you were okay."

"I'm okay. Look I know you said there's nothing between you and LaDana but the way she acts says different."

"What about ole' boy that was ready to step to me about you? Is he your ex?"

"Yes, he's my ex but that's none of your business."

"None of my business? Since day one I've explained matters to you that technically weren't your business because we had just met. I still afforded you the respect of telling you to put your mind at ease because I'm trying to get to know you."

"I didn't ask you to do that Rohan."

"Can we talk about this inside please?"

"Not a good idea. I don't let strangers inside. You can be that killer their looking for on the news for all I know," she sarcastically shot back.

"Look woman! I'm trying to get to know you but you're not giving me a chance because you have this preconceived notion that all men are the same. I'm nothing like you ex Zora," I pleaded with her.

"You sure seem to play the same games like him," she shot back.

I hung my head in defeat. It was impossible to get through to this woman. She had electric fences, booby traps and grenades surrounding her heart to protect it.

"You really handle situations immaturely to be so educated. Conversation is the foundation of any relationship."

"First of all, this isn't a relationship and communication is the key to the foundation of a relationship not conversation."

"You just have it all figured out don't you? You know what; I'm going to let you have it. I'm a good man Zora and I'm done trying to convince you that I am. You enjoy your day Ms. Lady," I walked off not waiting for a response.

I was over her being so problematic for no good reason. Besides, I needed to get home to start dinner for my family.

We had a rule. No takeout and the host had to cook. Everyone brought a dish and engaged in copious conversation.

I was the only one who was that target because I was still single with no kids. Esdee was the oldest and she's thirty-eight and has been married fifteen years. She's a psychologist and as cynical as they come. Deliana is thirty-six and has been married for six years. She was so wild we're still trying to figure out how Kevin broke in that wild horse. Chalise is the youngest of the girls but two years older than me. She's thirty-four and is getting married this year. She was the mediator of the group. If she didn't know you, she appears quiet and shy but to us she's just as outspoken as the rest of us.

Ding Dong.

I looked down at my watch. My family had started to arrive early. The amazing thing about Wisconsin is that we have all four seasons.

Our summers are not really that hot normally so it's always a beautiful day to throw something on the grill and I won't be stuck with a lot of dishes.

Of course, Esdee was the first to arrive. She was adamant about being punctual and events starting on time.

"Hey baby brother. How are you?" She kissed me on the cheek and handed me her famous gooey macaroni and cheese.

"I'm good and you?" I asked walking the dish to the kitchen. "Where's Nathan?"

"He's working per usual. Why are you not done grilling? We supposed to be ready to eat by six?"

"Because I ran late at the shop today and you know I'm still doing repairs. I have some help so it should be done sooner than I expected."

"Who did you hire? Did you go with my recommendation?"

"No."

I was being vague on purpose. I didn't need Esdee all up in my business she could con anything out of your head.

"Well, as long as it gets done," she shrugged.

I was relieved she had left the conversation alone.

Within half an hour the entire family had arrived.

They all sat around talking and drinking while I finished grilling.

"Make sure that meat don't touch my grilled veggies Ro!" Chalise demanded.

"Girl, I don't know how you a vegan when mama raised us on pork and chicken," I laughed taking a swig of my beer.

"We're allowed to evolve Ro. Just make sure my food right son."

"I'm not your son! I keep telling you that."

"Boy bye."

"Leave your brother alone," my mother told her.

"Yes ma'am," she agreed but stuck her tongue out when my mother went back to her conversation with my father.

I returned the favor but got caught.

"Rohan stop taunting your sister," my mom said.

"Yes ma'am."

Chalise smiled in victory. We're closer in age so she's always been a pest for as long as I could remember.

"Rohan when are you going to get a woman? You know if a man ain't married by the time he at least turns thirty-two the perception is that something is wrong with him," Deliana laughed.

She was already on her second sex on the beach. I made those drinks strong as hell so I know she was feeling it.

I ignored her as if I couldn't hear her over the Maze and Frankie Beverly being Bluetooth through the sound system.

"You know you heard me Ro!" She yelled louder forcing everyone's eyes to turn to me.

"Look, mind your business."

"I'm just saying. Why haven't you brought LaDana around lately? We met her that one time at the park and haven't seen her since. We all agreed we like her," she smiled looking around at my sisters and mom.

"LaDana is too audacious for my liking. I need a woman that understands that I'm the man."

"What are we back in prehistoric times? I guess you want to be able to knock her out and drag her back to the cave by her hair for sex when you feel like it huh?"

"Stop being sarcastic you know what I mean."

"Why are men so intimidated by the twenty-first century woman? Is our education, higher paying jobs and sexual confidence that much of an issue to the men in society?" Esdee chimed in.

"No, they just want to grab us by the pus-" Deliana put her hand over her mouth once she remembered mom was sitting right across from her glaring in disapproval.

"Can y'all chill?"

"Yeah, leave that man alone," Kevin spoke up.

I was glad one of them spoke up. My dad was accustomed to us being outnumber by my mom and sisters and felt he was too old to be arguing with them at this point.

"Our brother is an amazing asset to any woman. We just want to make sure he's putting himself out there," Chalise rebutted.

"I am. I've been trying to get this woman to give me a chance. She's just complex and hard to get close to."

"Oh, really? Who is this woman?" Esdee asked.
My stomach was two stepping at the thought of telling my judgmental sisters that Zora was the one I was running behind.

"It's a woman named Zora."

"Zora. Why does that name sound familiar?" Esdee's brows were wrinkled as she thought about the name. "Ain't that the girl who stole from you?" She blurted out.

"Who told you that?" I asked.

"Oh, hell no!" Deliana waive her hands as if she was an umpire declaring a player safe at the home plate.

I just rolled my eyes and they started to rant about how she wasn't good enough.

"Ro, she's already giving out red flags. I ain't trying to be around anyone who steals. I ain't got time to be hiding my purse when I come around you," Chalise laughed but she was being serious.

"Mommy, what you think?" Esdee asked looking for her to co-sign on the census.

"He's grown," was all she said causing my sisters mouth to drop.

"Ma, really?" Deliana laughed.

"I'm not getting in his personal life anymore. If we leave him alone, he might just find someone to marry and give me a grandbaby with," she took another sip of her tea.

"One last thing and I will leave it alone," Esdee said. "I know you said LaDana can be a bit aggressive Ro, but maybe that's the type of woman you need. You have a strong personality and an overly sensitive woman can't handle that. You can be intense at times.

You need someone who can stand up under that type of pressure."

They all nodded in agreement including my mom. The men had long run out leaving me to the wolves to watch the game. Wimps.

With that being said, the conversation was dead, at least for now. I'm sure I would get several text messages warning me to stay away from Zora.

My sisters were right. Zora was giving me all kids of red flags and I was ignoring them. I have my own commitment phobias so I don't need someone I have to force to see the man I am.

Maybe I should reconsider what's right in front of me.

LADANA

I was still feeling some type of way about Rohan's rejection. He insisted on going against the grain and I wasn't happy at all about it.

Esdee assured me yesterday she would handle it when I texted her. I also told her about the exchange in front of Ro's store with Zora and that thug.

"Good morning LaDana," I didn't notice that Rohan had pulled up to open his store the same time I showed up to open the coffee shop.

Honestly, I was tired of chasing his ass and was hell bent on dodging him.

"You are really bi-polar you know that?"

"I'm sorry if I was rude yesterday. Can I make it up to you by taking you to dinner?"

"Are you serious right now? You snap on me about respecting your boundaries and being too aggressive now you want to take me out? Yeah, whatever. I'll respectfully decline," I gave him the side eye while walking in the shop.

He followed behind to plead his case.

"Dana, let me make it up to you. Please."

I tapped my fresh set of French tips on the counter as I considered his offer.

"Okay."

"Great. I'll pick you up at eight. Do you still live in the same place?"

"Yes I do."

"Awesome. It's a date then."

"A date? Uh-huh."

"What?"

"Nothing. We'll see how it goes."

"Well, you have a great day and thank you for the opportunity," he flashed me those pearly whites.

I watched him walk away thinking of all types of nasty things I would do to his fine ass.

Rohan was going to be my husband whether he realized it or not. By the way things are going I think he sees that I'm what's best for him.

The day couldn't go by fast enough. Before I knew it, I was speeding down North Park Street.

I already had the perfect dress in mind.

Once I was home I showered and slipped into my black satin spaghetti strap knee length dress.
It compliments my best assets and I was sure Rohan wouldn't be able to keep his hands off me.

I heard a knock at the door but decided to wait a few extra seconds because I already knew it was Rohan.

I didn't want to appear too eager.

"Wow," Rohan drooled as his eyes traveled the length of my body.

I smiled modestly as if I didn't already know I could grab any man's attention I wished.

"Thank you. Let me grab my purse and I'll be ready."

He held the door open to his Audi.

"You're always listening to this old school music," I teased. "You know we do have some current artist with music that can give you the same vibe?"

"I know I just prefer old school. Something wrong with that?" He smiled.

I swear every time he smiled my panties got a little wet.

I just wanted to lick the sweat from his six pack to quench my thirst.

Rohan opened my door and handed the valet his keys once we pulled up to Johnny Delmonico's Steakhouse.

It had an old school but upscale vibe to it. I personally preferred the Tornado Steak House but if I'm with Rohan I could care less.

The waiter came to the table and took our drink orders.

"We will have a bottle of red wine for the table," Rohan decided for us without asking my preference.

If he had bothered asking he would've known I preferred white wine.

"I will actually have a glass of white wine please," I corrected Rohan's order.

"My apologies. I should've asked. Red wine is normally better with steak but everyone has different tastes buds."

He wasn't offended which made me relieved. He could be set in his ways and extremely old school.

"So how is the progress going with your Masters?" He asked me.

I was shocked he remembered. I held down two jobs and went to school. It had me in tears on more occasions than I cared to admit. I was busting my butt to pay off my school loans while I was in school. I also secured several scholarships which made that goal extremely feasible.

The way I calculated I should have what I borrow to complete my degree paid off around six months after I was out of school.

My primary job has already guaranteed me a higher paying position once I graduate.

I was maintaining a 4.0 GPA and on the Dean's List.

"School is going great. I'm right on track to graduate this year and I can't wait! I'll be making an extra twenty-thousand a year with my masters at my current job," I bragged.

Hell, I worked hard and someone deserved to hear that I was the shit with no toilet paper might I add.

"That's amazing. Black, educated and beautiful which are all exceptional qualities in a woman."

His compliment caused me to blush.

"Unlike that riff raff you've been allowing to come into your shop. Not to pass judgement but it seems like you're out of her league."

"A person's social status doesn't make them out of your league. I personally like to get to know a person prior to passing judgement. Life can be unkind enough. We don't need to echo that same energy with each other."

"I'm not being unkind; I'm just stating facts. The few times I've seen her next door have been in the same pants with different shirts. It explains why she's a thief. You're brave allowing her to come back after what she did. Then that fiasco in front of your bookstore with her little boy toy was crazy."

"I brought you out to dinner to spend time with you not to bash Zora. Let's change the subject because I'm losing my appetite."

Here he goes again taking up for this girl he barely knew. What made her so special?

We made small talk the rest of dinner but I could tell Rohan was just being cordial. He opted out of dessert so we could leave earlier.

He was extremely moody to be a man. Anything set him off but I wasn't giving up just yet.

"Would you like to come in for a night cap?" I offered.

What I really want to say was let me swallow that ten-inch python resting on your thigh.

"No, I should get home. I have to open the shop early to finish the repairs. I'm almost done," he forced a fake smile.

"Rohan, I didn't mean to go after Zora. I'm just protective of you and I feel it was perceived wrong. I wasn't attacking her I was defending you."

"I understand," he lied.

His eyes betrayed him. I could see the disappointment staring back at me through his deep-set bedroom eyes.

"I truly hope so. You know how I feel about you and I'm glad you gave me the chance to have some one on one time with you. See you tomorrow Rohan," I kissed him on the cheek. "I hope that was okay but you were the one who said it was a date. At the end of the said date normally comes a kiss," I shifted my weight nervously in my heels causing my right shoe to jerk to the right.

"It was fine. I will see you in the morning LaDana. Thank you for your time on this evening."

I watched him walk back to his car and wait until I was all the way inside before he left.

I can't afford any more foolish mistakes if I was serious about Rohan being mine. Tonight would be the last time I ever spoke on Zora to him.

I ran inside to give Esdee the update on Rohan and me. She's been coaching me on winning her brother over.

Once she told me that my name came up at family dinner, I was geeked. If the mom and sisters liked you that meant half the work was done in making that man yours.

If I was a betting woman my money would be on me.

JILLIAN

"When did you start back cracking your bones in your fingers? You only use to do that when you were stressed. Is something wrong?" Elliot asked.

"Honey, do you think I can go back to teaching?"

I felt like my heart was going to jump out of my chest and start dancing on the table.

Elliot rarely told me no. He adjusted the glasses on his face giving what I'd ask careful consideration.

"Why do you want to go back to work babe? Are you not happy being at home anymore?"

"I love being here for you and the kids but I think I'm ready to get back out there. Maybe even half a day or as a substitute teacher to get my feet wet. The kids are in school all day now and I'm just here anyway."

"You're here making sure we have a hot meal, clean clothes and the right energy in our home. I would never stop you from having a career but I just thought being here for us was fulfilling you."

"It does. I just been noticing you stressing lately when you handle the finances and I want to help El. We are a team and I don't want you to feel you have to shoulder this weight on your own."

I started to cry not because of the thought of him being stressed but because I've never kept anything from Elliot. We were best friends and we promised before we got married we would never lose that part of us.

Another baby didn't fit into the picture right now and the notion of killing a part of him without his consent was ripping away at my conscious.

"Baby, I got us. We are good I promise. You have access to all the accounts, stocks, mutual funds the whole shebang. You talking like we are a paycheck away from living under the bridge and that's not the case."

"El, the kids are in private school, we have the mortgage and both car notes. The just the tip of the iceberg of the debt we have monthly."

Elliot just smiled the way he always did that seemed to calm my restless mind.

I've never seen him sweat or spaz out. He's never even raised his voice at me not once.

He's this gentle soul that I was blessed to find in a sea of fuckboys.

El was a rare find and I would do anything to protect him...even sacrifice a fetus we couldn't afford at the time.

If Zora knew I thought of this baby as a fetus she would flip her top. To her a heartbeat meant life but I hold the rights to my body and will do what I think is best. Before now you couldn't get me to support abortion but now that the shoe is on the other foot I needed to lace it up and see this through.

"Where did you just go?" He asked shattering my daze.

"Nowhere just pondering on what I just said."

"We've had no major changes in our finances in over two years. Where is all of this coming from Jilly?"

"I just worry sometimes. You know how I get baby. I will just feel better adding to our nest egg a bit more that's all."

"Well, it's up to you. Just let me know what you want to do."

"Thank you," I place my hand on his knee prior to heading into the kitchen.

"It must be Jilly 'cause jam don't shake like that. Baby your butt looks bigger and them hips are spreading something serious," he smacked my butt as I passed.

"Boy!"

I was praying he wouldn't figure it out. I was starting to gain weight and I need to decide fast about this baby.

He licked his lips and I remembered how I got this new bulge in my stomach.

Elliot gave boy next door nerd vibes with his glasses, neat fade and tea colored skin. His almond shaped eyes and high cheek bones were often obstructed by his glasses.

He watched me until and disappeared into the kitchen. Have you ever had someone look at you as if you could do no wrong?

Me either.

It was one of the reasons I could alter our perfect life. We finally have it figured out. We worked so many hours in the beginning of our marriage to get to this point.

Some days when I was coming home from work, he was leaving. Pulling long hours just to secure the foundation we have now.

Taking crap from those people on his job who were intimated by his creative genius with only one goal which was making sure we never ended back on rock bottom.

Yep. We've seen rock bottom. I was done with my teaching degree but Elliot was still pursuing his master's in accounting.

We were getting our food from and pantry and barely keeping the lights on. I refused to go back to that.

ZORA

I paced back and forth across my cold wood floors sipping on my glass of wine. Rohan caught me off guard when he popped up at my house yesterday. Since then I haven't been able to get him off my mind. LaDana is persistent but he has been clear that he does not want her. I should at least give him a chance but I know at this point he is over my mood swings.

We have the poetry slam coming up I could use that as an excuse to reach out to him.

After I've pondered it more, I took a deep breath and called Rohan.

The bravado of his voice pulsated my heart strings.

This could be my chance at something real. It was unexpected but what if it changed my life for the better.

I haven't heard from Sobray since the incident at the bookstore so I think he finally got the picture that we're done.

"Hello."

"Hi, it's Zora. How are you?"

"What a pleasant surprise. You mean to tell me you actually saved my number I gave you?"

"Yes I did. We do have to make sure this poetry slam goes off without a hitch. I can't let you have me out here looking bad."

"You looking bad, huh?"

"Yes, that's what I said," I laughed.

Come to think about it, I laughed a lot when I was in contact with him.

"Well, if you have time, I can come pick you up so we can finalized the last of the plans if you would like."

"You don't have to pick me up. It's only a few blocks. I'll get dressed and head your way."

"Okay, see you when you get here. If you change your mind call me so I can pick you up."

"Yes, since you done blew up my spot."

"I had to let you know what was up woman," he laughed. "You're more slippery than a fish out of water."

"Yea, yea. See you in a bit."

"Okay," he said ending the call.

I've been working extra hours at work to get ahead and get me a few outfits.

I pulled my box braids up into a bun and moisturized my lips with a tinted lip gloss.

Between shifts I did my own hair to save money. I started with the perimeter and worked my way in. It wasn't like I had a full list of things to do once I was off work.

I didn't mind being alone it was peaceful.

A notification went off on my phone and I figured it was Rohan wondering where I was. Getting ready was taking longer than expected.

When I opened my messages, I was disappointed to see that it was my mom again.

We've been conversation via text for a few weeks trying to get our relationship back on track but I was hesitant. I already had full plate.

My mom looked better when I saw her awhile back but I had no way of knowing if she had kicked her habit.

Every daughter longed for her mother and if she was clean, I didn't want to miss out on this opportunity.

We've been working up to her coming over for dinner but I was still a bit skittish.

I sent her a quick text that I would call her once I got back in for the evening.

I threw my phone in my purse and headed out. With each step my heart pounded to rhythm of its own.

"You finally made it," Rohan said.

I eyed his broad chest protruding like boulders from his black shirt that read 'Black King'.

Yeah you are. I thought to myself.

"Yes, sorry I'm running later than expected.

"It's quite alright. Follow me."

He led me to the area I normally hid in to read. He had candles lit and champagne on ice. Two white plates trimmed in gold had salmon and broccoli.

"What is this?"

"Well, it looks like you're never going to allow me to take you out so I had to improvise. Zora I'm a great man. I know exactly what I want and it's you."

"You don't even know me."

"Well, sit down and let's change that."

I could no longer fight the way I felt for this man. I couldn't deny the chemistry between us.

"So, tell me something that no one knows about you."

"Just jumping right in are we?"

I nervously shifted in my favorite seat at his question. Things that people don't know about you is the usually stuff you don't want to tell.

"Yes we are. If you hadn't made me corner you, I could've allowed pleasant conversation to reveal everything I wanted to know about you."

"Well, I'm an only child."

"I'm sure people know that about you Zora. Nice try but give me the real. You know what? I'll go first." He took a sip from his glass and continued, "My fiancé called off our wedding a week before it was supposed to happen."

"Are you serious?"

"Yep," he leaned back into his chair and folded his arms. "She said she refused to settle and that I lacked the proper drive to match her hustle. I found it funny that she was on social media the day our wedding was supposed to take place with another man already. It's safe to say she was sleeping with him the entire time."

"That's cold."

"Well, I was able to get most of my money back and open my shop. This shop saved me when I thought I was going to lose my mind. I put everything I had in her so there was no backup plan or side piece waiting to ease the pain. I threw myself in this bookstore and one day I didn't hurt anymore. And you? Who hurt you?"

I tossed my head back while running my fingers through my fro.

"I've never been in love before. I've gone from one foster home to another since I was five. Once I aged out of the system, I became homeless. I had to steal to put clothes on my back and food in my stomach. I wasn't proud of it but I was just trying to survive from one day to the next. The book...that I stole." I was embarrassed to even speak on it again to him face to face but we're being transparent with one another right now and I couldn't fold. I was doing well at allowing Rohan in. "It was the only thing my mother bought me before I was taken from her. It was a birthday gift. The words were well beyond my reading level but I learned quickly. When my ex refused to give me the replacement copy I found I was devastated. When I found a copy at your store, I had to have it but I couldn't afford it."

"I see," he said.

"As far as my ex goes...he was there when I needed a place to stay. It treated me horribly but he was my...first so I was attached to him. He's the only man I ever been intimate with so it's been hard up until recently to keep him out of my life."

"I can understand how bad loving the wrong person can damage and change you. It will never judge you or lie to you. I'm just trying to be whatever you need and show you how to be loved the right way."

No one has ever done anything so thoughtful for me. I was stuck sitting there trying to process my emotions.

"Are you nervous about the poetry slam coming up?"

"Nervous as a black man being stopped in the middle of the night by a police officer on a dark road. If I lose this shop, I don't know what I'll do Zora. It's all I have left."

"You won't. You really need to give yourself more credit. You have the only black owned bookstore in Madison, Wisconsin. You need to market and monopolize on that. You got this! Reach out to some of the other business owners in the area and collab on some events. Stop shrinking yourself because someone made you feel unworthy at one point. You're more than enough."

"And you wonder why I pursue you so intensely."

I smiled and sipped more on my champagne.

"Aren't you a busy bee?" LaDana was like a foot fungus. No matter if you pissed on it, it still manages to grow back after a while.

"What are you doing here LaDana?"

"I saw the lights on and thought you were burning the after-hour oil with the repairs. I was going to offer my aid but I see you have help. It's not as nice as the restaurant you took me to last night but it doesn't look like it takes much to satisfy her," she cut her eyes at me.

I was over her mess and Rohan were about to see my other side.

"LaDana you're way out of line!" Rohan raised his voice for the second time around me.

"No she's fine. Desperation is unbecoming of her but I'm guessing it's why you have a hard time letting her down. Apparently, you're giving her hope so I'll let you both hash this out while I excuse myself."

"You're not leaving, she is!" Rohan stood to block my path. "LaDana, yes we went out last night only because I frustrated that I possibly blew my chance with Zora. I don't want you and last night confirmed that. You have no humility or grace about yourself and it's exhausting."

"Your sisters also told me that they don't want you with that thief over there! Wait until I tell them this shit."

"I don't give a damn what you tell them! I'm a grown ass man! Get the hell out of my store."

I waited until LaDana stomped out of the store to address what I just heard.

"Your family knows about me stealing the book?"

"It's not like that. LaDana has her claws in my sisters so she goes back and tells them my business."

"If we made this official, they would only see me now as a thief. They wouldn't try to get to know me because in their minds I'm already unworthy of your love."

His silence told me everything I needed to know. I grabbed my purse and left not bothering to give him the chance to come up with another water down excuse.

"At least take the food Zo."

"My name is Zora and no thank you Rohan. I've lost my appetite."

Not only were my feelings hurt I was humiliated to know that his family knows about one of my weak moments.

I could never be with him knowing how close he is to his family and what they think of me.

This is exactly why I stay to myself. It's always something with Rohan. From what I saw tonight he's leading me and LaDana on telling us the same lies. I tried giving him the benefit of the doubt and look what it got me.

This Negro actually had me on a date after he was just on one the day prior with LaDana.

Talking about he's different. He aight'.

I fussed at myself the entire way home for telling him so much about myself. Only Jilly knows about my past and he didn't deserve that part of me.

If I hurried home I could still catch my shows on T.V.

*   *   *

Rohan has been blowing me up for two days now. The Poetry slam is today and he was on his own. His problems are no longer mine.

He finally left a voicemail and I decided to listen to what he had to say.

"Zora, I know you're mad at me and I can't blame you. When I went out with LaDana I realized why I haven't pursued her or gave in to her aggressive flirtation. She's not what I want. I know you don't believe that I want to be with you but can you at least come to the poetry slam? I can't do this without you. Please come tonight."

Rohan always had an excuse for the disarray between him and LaDana. If he wasn't interested in her why would he go out with her? He must have some type of feelings for her. I mean she's already in good with his family who now think I'm a thief to put the icing on the cake.

I pushed Rohan out of my mind as I waited on my mother to arrive. We've finally been able to align our schedules for dinner.

I needed to focus on what mattered. I was swearing off me for now.

I was glad she was doing well. When we speak on the phone, she's so clear headed these days.

Knock. Knock.

I heard a light tap on the door and I knew it was my mom.

"Jilly? What are you doing here?"

"I can't do it Z," she cried. "I can't kill our baby. We've always wanted a baby girl and what if this is her?" She rubbed her still flat stomach.

"Come in," I embraced her and then pulled her inside.

She took a seat at the table while I returned to cooking.

"Want something to drink?"

"No. I just stopped by to settle my nerves so that I can tell Elliot. He also agreed to let me start back teaching again too," she smiled.

"See, it's all working out. You got this baby girl."

"You expecting company? I haven't seen you in this kitchen since you moved here," she teased.

Warmth filled my chest when I thought of the possibility of rekindling my relationship with my mother.

"My mother is coming over for dinner today."

"Awweee! I'm so happy for you Z," she jumped up to wrap her tiny arms around my full waist.

"Thank you. I'm nervous. I'm not sure what I will say to her or what I will be like to actually see her in person."

"Y'all are just getting back on track so keep it light for now. Don't dive into the heavy stuff out the gate," she suggested lifting the lids on my pots.

"Get out of my pots Jilly," I shooed her away.

"I'm eating for two now let me get some of those greens girl."

"Grab you a bowl. The Louisiana hot sauce is in the cabinet which you don't need. Going to burn my god baby eyes out," I gave her a stern look as she doused her bowl in the red concoction.

"Hey what's this you're working on?" She opened my red notebook that was bulging due to my pen being nestled in the spine.

"No, don't read that Jilly!" I snatched my book from her.

"Is that poem for Rohan," she bit down on the tip of the fork rotating her tongue through the slits.

"Mind your business! You know if sensitive about my shit," I stuck my tongue out at her on my way to put my book away.

"So, what's been going on with you and him?"

"Not a damn thing. Can you believe he invited me to the shop? When I got there he had a candlelit dinner waiting on me?"

"What?! You been holding out?"

"I know you've been going through your own thing. I didn't want to keep bothering you with this mess. I mean it's really nothing. We just can't seem to get on the same page. Every time I take the leap here comes LaDana to remind me that she's lurking in the shadows," I leaned against the cabinet folding my arms across my chest.

My flesh prickled at the thought of the deviant.

"Umm, who is LaDana?"

"The coffee girl that works next door that's always popping up at the most inopportune times. I told you about her! He insists there's nothing between them but the way she acts I wonder."

"Friend, we could've been beat her up! Rohan give me good vibes. I like his aura," she waived her hands wildly around her head.

"Girl…to be honest I really think he's out of my league. He seems to have it all figured out. What if I fall for him and he sees how much of a mess I am and leaves me? People are good at abandoning me ya' know," my throat clenched with despair just saying it out loud.

"Come and sit down," Jilly rested her chin on her entwined fingers.

"Rohan is not your mom or Sobray. You've been doing the work to deal with your childhood imprints but it's still a process. I wish you could see what everyone around you does Z. Let this man love you. Don't be afraid to fight for what you know you want deep down."

"It's too early to be fighting for anyone. We're not even in a relationship."

"Only because you let every little thing scare you off. If he didn't care he wouldn't keep explaining himself to you. And you probably only took that girl out because you keep tripping!"

"Jilly you know her being in good with his family is a big deal."

"It's only because they don't know you yet."

"Oh, they know I stole that book from his store so they all think I'm a thief."

"Ohhh," Jilly mouthed cutting her eyes over to me as I stirred my greens more.

"See!"

Jilly's confirmation just made me want to die on the spot.

"I stand by what I said. Once they meet you I'm sure they will fall in love with you."

"I don't know why we're still talking about him. I shut him down the other night and I've been ignoring his calls."

"Yes, but you're still over here writing poems about him soooo."

"So nothing. It's how I process my feelings. Just because I write about him doesn't mean that I'm still feeling him with his chiseled jawline, thick beard and his deep-set eyes."

"Do you need to change your panties before your mama get here," Jilly burst into laughter.

"Girl, I'm just staying. I've never said he wasn't fine as all get out. Lord help your people because I be lusting something serious every time I'm in his presence."

Ding Dong.

I went to the door and my heart sank when I saw my mother standing in front of me. She was holding my favorite desserts sweet potato pie.

"Well, let me get out of y'all hair," Jilly said.

"Mom, this is Jillian Adams. She's my best friend in the whole world."

My mother extended her hand, "Pleased to meet you my name is Sabrina."

"Nice meeting you! I look forward to getting to know you. I will call you later Z," she said making her exit.

"You can have a seat at the table mom. Dinner is ready."

"Thank you. Where should I put the pie?"

"Just sit it on the table."

I place the serving dishes I bought at a garage sale awhile back on the table.

"Everything smells so delicious."

"Thanks mama."

"You're welcome."

"So, how have you been?"

"I've been well. Just staying out of trouble. They finally gave me my disability so that helps. My rent going to go up but that's okay. It'll be nice having some more income come in."

"Yeah, I can understand that. I work so many hours I don't know whether I'm coming or going but at least I finally have my own place. I was staying wherever I could for a while."

"I'm sorry baby. I can't imagine how hard life was growing up in foster care. I tried to get you back but they felt I wasn't stable enough to."

What she meant was that she was a drug addict and wouldn't get clean to get me back.

I was choking on my anger with every word she spoke. I knew my mother would be a trigger for me but I needed to face this part of my past so I could move forward.

Always wondering what life would've been like with her has plagued me for years.

I needed to extend grace to her so she can show me that she is ready to be the mother that I've longed for.

"I understand mama. Did you have any other kids after me?"

She was eerily quiet.

"Mama?"

"You had a brother that was younger than you. He got pneumonia and died. Where is your bathroom?"

Her countenance changed. It was as if all the color had left her cheeks.

I waited patiently but after twenty minutes I got worried.

"Mama?" I tapped on the bathroom door but there was no answer.

My bathroom door didn't lock so I peeked in to check on her.

"Are you kidding me?!"

My mom was barely lucid on the toilet with a needle still stuck in her arm.

Raged poisoned my veins as flashes from my childhood drowned me in the bathroom doorway.

I thought she was clean! She looked clean! She sounded clean!

There was no point in trying to get any sense into her until her high wore off.

I slid down the wall in the bathroom and cried like I was five years old again.

I sat there for hours until she finally creeped out.

"Zora...I...I...I'll just go."

"Yes, do that."

My eyes were swollen shut from crying so hard. I watched my mother walk out on me as she had so many times. Once again, she chose what she loved more than anything in this world. Drugs.

Ksshhh! Kssshh!

I threw the used dishes still filled with food against the walls and floor.

Ding Dong.

"What?!"

Jilly was shocked at my response.

"What's going on? I forgot my purse on the couch. I had to come all the way back to get it. Z, what's wrong?"

"She did it again Jilly," I collapsed in her arms in devastation.

"What do you mean?"

"I walked in the bathroom and she was high out of her mind. I just sat outside of the bathroom crying until her high came down. I was that helpless five-year-old girl again," I started to hyperventilate.

"Calm down Z. I got you," she started to cry too.

She sat there holding me for hours as I cried myself to sleep.

"Oh my god Jilly, Elliot is going to kill you. It's morning!"

"No, I texted to him about what happened so he understood. He said the kids were already sleep anyway when I came back to get my purse and he was just up late working. I wasn't going to leave you in the state you were in."

"I'm sorry friend. Thank you so much," I hugged her.

"Well, me and this baby gotta eat so can you we clean up this food art you have splattered all around this kitchen?"

"I got you baby mama. When are you going to tell Elliot about the baby?"

"Today," she smiled. "I have a feeling everything is going to be just fine," she assured me.

"I told you."

We cleaned, ate and Jilly left to tell her husband they had baby number three on the way.

JILLIAN

I was a ball of emotion as I made my way home to my husband. I was done toiling over my decision to keep my baby or not but I still wasn't sure how Elliot would respond.

"Good morning baby. How is Z holding up?"

"She's good considering. How are the boys? Are they up yet?"

"Yes, I took them to your mother's. She wanted to spend the day with them. She said something about a homemade drive in she set-up for them in the backyard or something."

"Oh, that's sounds fun."

"I know right. I wonder if my long legs can fit inside one of those cardboard boxes," he joked.

"Baby, I need to tell you something. Let's sit down."

"Girl, you ain't leaving me are you?"

"Boy stop being silly! I'm pregnant."

"I know."

"What do you mean you know?"

"Woman I know your body better than you. Why you think I slapped your butt the other day. Girl when you carry my kids you get thicker and wetter in all the right places. When you asked about going to work, I knew you were worried if we could financially support another baby."

"Why you make me sweat then?" I playfully punched him in the arm.

"Because I wanted you to talk to me Jilly. We won't be one of those couples who hide things and fight battles individually only to be destroyed. If we face it all together then we can overcome anything. You don't have to work unless you want to. We're good babe. We're great. I got a promotion!"

"Babe, stop playing with me!"

"I'm not. That's why I've been working the long hours. It hasn't been because of financial issues; it was because I was doing everything in my power to secure this new position."

"You're such and amazing man. I'm blessed that God made me your rib."

"All I do is for you and our kids. I will forever protect y'all and keep you safe. My family is my world and you are my muse baby. Now let's go have some nasty hot sex."

"Well, it's not like I can get pregnant. Hopefully you got me a baby girl cooking in here this time. Tired of a house full of stinky socks and sports."

"Come on and let me thank you properly," he smiled swooping me up in his arms.

"Aht aht! You promised me nasty sex so come and bend me over this kitchen counter!"

"Don't mind if I do."

The passion, lust and love in my husband's eyes made my fear of having another child by him seem so crazy now.

As he undressed me, I remembered all the reasons I fell in love with this man.

ROHAN

I was growing nervous by the minute as I went over my guest list for my first poetry slam. I had an overwhelming response from the surrounding community. I was currently on my way to our local radio station here in Madison to do one last promo for tonight's show.

"Mr. Jefferson, you can come back now. We're ready for you."

I stuffed my list back in my bag and followed the petite white lady through the double glass doors.

"Take a seat man. Thank you for coming in today."

"Thank you for having me. I really appreciate this opportunity. I've been on edge trying to think about what I should say," I confessed.

"Let it come natural. People can sense when you're pulling their legs. So my staff said you're hosting your first poetry slam and open mic night. Upon researching you bookstore I learned that you own the only black owned bookstore in Madison. That's something awesome!"

Fish had red hair solidifying his Irish roots. His pale skin had a bit of a tan from the nice summer days we've been enjoying. He leaned back in his chair with admiration. He shifted his average build in front of his mic once we got the que that we would be going live on the air in a matter of minutes.

"You're tuned in to Mornings with Fish, this is your boy Fish and we have Rohan Jefferson here in the studio today. He's the owner of Knowledge is Power Bookstore here in Madison. The ONLY black owned bookstore in the city," he stressed only.

"Thank you Fish I'm elated to be in the building."

"So word on the street is that you're having a poetry slam and open mic going on tonight at your bookstore. Tell us more about that."

"I wanted to bring a different flavor to the night scene her in the city. We have an amazing melting pot of different cultures and I want to showcase that. Words have the power to change lives. It's one of the reasons I opened my bookstore."

"So will we hear from you tonight?"

"Maybe," I laughed. "No, I'm not really into writing. I just love to hear the thoughts of others though. I need everyone in the city to come on out and drop some knowledge."

"There you have it guys. Make sure to get down to Knowledge is Power and tell Rohan that Fish sent ya'."

Once we were confirmed to be off the air. I thank Fish once again for the opportunity and rushed off.

I looked at my phone and still no response from Zora.

At this point she was just being childish. This was her idea. How could she fold on me at a time like this? We agreed to do this together. I don't know what the hell I'm doing.

I went along with it because it seemed like a good idea but I really was leaning on her to make this work.

I thought we would have people come out but I'm turning people away at this point and putting together a waitlist in case someone cancels.

I have a minimum capacity at the shop but if tonight is an indication of what's in store for the future I would be able to buy the abandoned studio upstairs and expand.

Never in a million years would such a thought cross my mind. I was barely keeping the doors open but here I was contemplating growth. All because of Zora's idea.

I was reminded of her telling me that I was more than capable of pulling this off.

Boss up Ro. You got this.

I opted to leave her one more message.

I listened on the other end as the phone rang over and over until I was prompted to leave a message.

"Zora, I know you're not speaking to me but I just want to thank you for the idea for the poetry night. If you're not busy I hope you can come by. We've had and awesome response. I actually just left the radio station to promote the event. I'm excited and nervous. It would be nice to have you by my side but I understand it's been a bit of a rocky start. Take care."

I hung up the phone at peace with this being the only closure that I may get from Zora. She's been consistently emotionally unavailable.

It's all for the best anyway. The last thing I need is to be suffocated by a relationship while I'm trying to rebrand and build my bookstore. I don't have time to keep running after Zora every time uncomfortable situations arise.

I made a quick stop by the store to make sure the event planner was setting things up to my standards.

I was going for a sexy sultry vibe. I even bought Hookahs and did some remodeling to make it more inviting in the bookstore.

Misty didn't disappoint. My vision had been brought to life perfectly.

My expresso machine was set-up and it would even have a server who would do fancy designs for the patrons tonight.

The hookahs were lined against the wall behind the counter with all the flavors.

"I still think it's a bad idea to have hookahs in a freakin' bookstore Ro," Misty complained.

"Between security and the servers we all should be able to keep an eye on everything. I mean we're not selling liquor so we have to at least provide some type of incentive. Don't forget the first two people get theirs complimentary," I reminded her.

"I know. I know," she rolled her eyes because I was working her last nerve with my nagging. "Go home and get ready so you can be on time. Your sisters have already been calling making sure I kick you out of here. They are so proud of you," she smiled.

"Well, let me get home before they call while I'm here. I don't have time to hear their mouths."

I couldn't wait to see how tonight unfolded.

I was home for about twenty minutes when the FedEx driver pulled up with a certified letter.

I opened it and it was a letter from my attorney. The trucking company finally agreed to pay my million dollars for my injuries in addition to pain and suffering.

Such a tremendous weight was lifted off of me. Now I could really enjoy the night without clocking how much money I have coming in. Wow! Now I can really take my bookstore to the next level and buy the space above me.

*   *   *

When I pulled up to the bookstore it was a line wrapped around the building. I was at a loss for words. I didn't know I had so much support in my city.

I greeted the patrons on the way in and once I was inside my mouth dropped. Misty has everything set up so nice.

Balloons matched the store décor. Candles and fresh flowers were systematically placed on the tables. She had a vendor come in that provided wine, which was okay. I really didn't want alcohol but it fit the current vibe and everyone in the building appeared to be on their grown and sexy.

My eyes lit up when I saw the bouncer turning in stacks of cash from the cover charge.

Misty even had the back patio set-up so we could take in more people. She moved from the big screen that was used inside the store for new releases and other announcements out there so they would be able to see the stage.

I was grinning from ear to ear.

"You like it?" Misty finally found me near my office.

"I love it! I can't thank you enough. You have no idea how much this means to me."

"I think I have an idea. You should've been doing this. The buzz on social media is that this is the new play for black creatives in the city."

"Wow!"

"I know, so you better just go ahead and hire me as a part of your staff."

"Let's see if we can make enough money in order for me to hire you."

"Hey brother," Deliana cooed dancing through the crowd. "Look at all of these people here to support!"

"I know! It's bananas!"

"Look who I brought with me."

My face quickly hardened when LaDana showed up behind my sister.

In an effort not to ruin my night I decided to play nice.

"Hello LaDana."

"Hi, Rohan. This is an amazing turn out. I'm so happy for you. I know this will be good for business."

"Yes, I'm hoping so. If you ladies will excuse me."

I got out of dodge just in case Zora walked in. I didn't want her to think I was still playing games with her heart.

I watched the door all night. Between sets we let old school music play while people networked.

As the night came to an end there was still no Zora. I checked my phone all night and she didn't even bother to respond to my voicemail.

In such a successful moment I felt so defeated.

"Leave that girl alone," Esdee interrupted me going through my phone.

"What are you talking about?"

"Baby brother I know you. You checking to see if that woman will call you."

"And what if I am?"

"You have a woman over there that is crazy about you that this family loves. You should give it a chance."

"She's not who I want and the more y'all push her on me the more I pull away. Now is not the time to get into this sis but thank you for coming."

I walked off leaving my sister where she stood. They didn't see the other sides of LaDana that I've been privy to.

"Oh, excuse me," I apologized to the woman I almost ran down getting away from my sister.

"No apologies necessary Rohan," she replied.

"Do I know you?"

"I'm Jillian, Zora's best friend. We're actually more like sisters."

"Did she send you? Is she okay?"

"She's okay and no she didn't send me. That stubborn mule would never," she laughed.

"Did you come for the open mic?"

"Yes and I want to give you something."

I watched as she pulled out a red notebook.

"She's going to kill me once she finds out I gave this to you. Just give it back to me once you're done so I can sneak it back in her apartment."

"What is this?"

"How she really feels about you. Zora has stacks of notebooks with poetry and stories that feed the soul and cause you to view life through her eyes."

"Why are you giving me this?"

"Because I feel you both are perfect for each other. She's been through a lot. She told me she told a bit of her past but just know everyone in her life has abandoned her except for me. She's terrified of love but I can't think of anyone on this planet who deserves to be loved the way she should."

"It's hard to get to know someone who takes flight at the first sight of trouble. She's not the only one who's been hurt in the past. Thank you for coming by. I will look this over. You can pick it up in the morning."

"Why don't you take it to her? I'll deal with the backlash."

"You sure that's a good idea?"

"I'm positive. Trust me."

I was hesitant about what Jillian had suggested until I opened to the last poem.

I think I love you but I'm afraid.
Afraid you will be an echo of my past.
Like what I've loved once that no longer exists.
In a world full of temporary satisfaction is anything built to last?
In a perfect world it would just be me and you.
Me having you all to myself.
Me alone with that smile, those kind words and that sexy physic

I want to love you but at times I struggle with loving myself.
If I were to be honest, I worry that one day you will stop loving me too.
You are like a breath of fresh air but at the same time so suffocating.
What if I start to love you so until I can't breathe without you?
Then you leave…

It was too late to go to her house but it was going to kill me if I waited until morning. I could use the notebook as an excuse to drop by.

I stood on the outside of her door chewing on the inside of my bottom lip wondering am I making a mistake.

I couldn't deny the connection I felt with Zora. Despite our inability to get out of our own way we still were like magnets to one another.

I'm convinced that she's the best thing that could happen to me.

Swallowing the lump in my throat I knocked on Zora's door.

"What are you doing here this time of night? Is everything okay?"

Zora looked different. She looked sad.

"I wanted to bring this back to you," I handed her the red notebook.

"How did you get this?"

"Jillian."

"I can't believe she would betray my trust like this! Did you read it?"

She was so upset I was damn near afraid to say that I did but I would never lie to her.

"Yes."

She rolled her eyes and walked away. I took it as a sign to come in.

Her apartment was modest but clean. It smelled of cinnamon and apple.

She threw the book on the couch and sat next to it.

"I'm not trying to play with your heart. We've both been through somethings and I know that we can love each other from a healthy place. I just want a real chance with you."

"What about your family? They think I'm a thief."

"I don't care about what they think. I will protect and defend you. I know they will love you just as much as I do once they get to know you. But this is about us not them."

"You…love…me?"

"I've loved you since the first day you came in my store and hid in the corner. It's not like you have a welcoming demeanor so I was intimated by you."

"You don't know me to love me."

"I know enough but I'm dying to know more. You're a once in a lifetime type of woman. I would be a fool to let you slip through my hands over misunderstandings. I will always fight for you."

Her face softened.

"Let me be here for you Zora. I don't want anything from you other than build you up and love you. I'm ready for love. Are you?"

"I don't know how," she whispered.

"I can teach you if you allow me."

"I have so much going on in my life right now. I don't know if it's a good time."

"How is it ever a bad time to be loved? Whatever is going on we can face it together. I ain't no punk woman," I laughed. "You might as well give in because I'm never letting you go Zora Mitchell.

"Let me show you something," she said.

I watched her go over to a large brown box. She pulled out notebook after notebook.

"I hope you don't have anywhere to be," she slid them over to me.

"There's no place I'd rather be."

Zora and I sat up until the wee hours of the morning as I read her work. I finally got her to agree to start publishing. I told her I would personally carry her books in my store.

I'm not sure how she ended up sleep on my chest but I've never felt a peace like it.

I pushed her hair back from her face and kissed her forehead. I held her tightly in my arms thanking God for allowing something so unexpected to change my life for the better.

ZORA

I was glad to have made it through another day of work. Rohan was adamant about picking me up, so I assumed my vibrating phone was him calling to let me know he was waiting outside. To my surprise, it was an unknown number. I usually didn't answer, but the twinge in my gut told me otherwise.

"Hello."

"Ms. Mitchell?"

"Yes...may I ask who is calling?"

"This is Dr. Bassin. I'm the emergency room doctor here at St. Mary's Hospital. We have your mother here, and we have you listed as an emergency contact. Can you come down to the hospital so that I can speak with you?"

"About what? Is she okay?"

"Yes, but she nearly overdosed. She's stable, but at some point, we need to release her to a family member to make sure she gets home okay."

At this point, I curled over with my hands on my knees, trying to wrap my head around what he was telling me.

"Okay, I will be there as soon as I can."

Seeing my mom in that condition in my bathroom made me resent her all over again.

I missed that connection with my mama. I just couldn't let her destroy me all over again.

I noticed Rohan's text, letting me know he was outside.

I started to choke on my tears. I was doing everything in my power to pull myself together. I didn't want Rohan to witness yet another drama-filled episode regarding my mother.

Pull it together, Zo. My steps were uncertain as I made my way to the bathroom. I had to clean my face before getting into the car.

I shot Rohan a quick message that I was on my way out. He responded, okay.

He was always patient when he waited for me to get off. He never complained, not once.

"Hey baby," I attempted to sound chipper.

"Hello, love. What's wrong?"

I couldn't hold it in any longer. I crumbled inside as the tears escaped.

"I got a call that my mother is in the emergency room. She almost overdosed."

"Oh, baby!" He embraced me. "It's going to be okay. Let's go check on her."

"I...I can't right now. I've had too many of these moments growing up, and I just can't today."

"I understand, but it's your mom Zo," he contended with me in an attempt to ignite my compassion.

"I wish I could, but this runs deeper than I care to explain right now."

"Okay. When you're ready, I want to be the one to take you."

"Okay," I lied to him for the first time.

I knew wholeheartedly that I wouldn't take him when I went to see my mother. I didn't want him seeing her like that.

I didn't need his pity or him thinking I was too weak to deal with my problems.

Rohan and I have been glued to the hip since he came to my place and declared how he felt about me. I must admit I was surprised, and his declaration came at a vulnerable moment in my life.

I haven't spoken to my mother despite her many phone calls, and text attempts to apologize.

To be honest, I was tired of her empty apologies. When I got the call from the hospital, it was one that I had dreaded since she came back into my life, and I discovered she was on drugs again.

Rohan has brought a new outlook on my life. I was already working on myself, and now I'm to the point where my worth is no longer negotiable.

My mother was the only person who reminded me otherwise.

What sane person would tie themselves to a woman who has an addict for a mother? An addict whom they may have to alter their plans for because she was self-destructive.

"You look like you about to pop girl," I teased Jilly, who I come by to take my mind off of my mother.

I didn't want her to worry about me and stress the baby.

Unbeknownst to her, this was just another play date with her boys. We sat in the park while they enjoyed the warm sun.

One thing I loved most about Wisconsin is that we get all four seasons. It gets frigid in the winters but the summers are perfect.

"Shut up. Everything is hurting me girl. I can't even laugh without farting. I'm sick of it," she laughed.

"How are you and Elliot?"

"We're great. With Elliot's promotion, I didn't have to go back to teaching, although I miss it at times. It's just getting too scary to be in a school with everything that's been going on. I'm extra paranoid about being pregnant. Every day I'm on the verge of a panic attack for little reasons. I want to pop this baby out and be on my way."

"On your way where silly," I nudged her.

"To my best post-pregnancy life."

"Well, you only have a few more months to go," I rubbed her belly, hoping I would feel my goddaughter move.

"At least it's a girl this time. Let's go shopping."

"We just went shopping yesterday. That girl has a closet full of stuff, and her nursery is overflowing already. We still have to make room for the stuff for your upcoming baby shower next month."

"I know I'm just so excited Z. I finally get my girl."

"I know, the third time was truly a charm."

"Yes, indeed."

You're the coffee that I need in the morning…

I looked down at my phone and saw it was my boo.

"Hey baby," I cooed into the phone. I was doing my best not to alarm Jilly that I was bothered by what's going on with my mom.

"Are you feeling better? I was worried about you," he asked.

Jilly pretended to stick her finger down her throat as if we were sickening her.

I just rolled my eyes and smiled. Jilly was thrilled that I finally found an emotionally and mentally whole man to date.

"I'm okay. Jilly came soon after you dropped me off. I'm trying to talk her out of going shopping again for this baby."

"Let her be great, baby," his baritone laughter echoed through my phone, causing Jilly to shake her head in agreement.

I was relieved he wasn't pressing the issue with my mother.

"No, sir. I have to keep her focused."

"Are we still on for dinner tonight? I know you have a lot going on right now."

"You know it. I'm looking forward to it. It will help me take my mind off things."

"Great. Hey, see if you can set something up in a few weeks with Jilly and Elliot. I would love to meet them both officially. I've met Jilly's crazy self, but I would like to meet her husband as well."

"Okay, I will ask her about it. I will see you later tonight, love."

"Okay. I'll pick you up at six."

"Cool beans," I said, ending the call.

"What? No, I love you yet?" Jilly volunteered for her unwarranted observation.

"We're not rushing into anything. We're just dating, trying to get to know one another. We haven't really made it official yet."

"Girl, he came to your house and declared how he felt. You were writing poetry about him before you even knew how he felt about you. Y'all are meant to be. Watch!"

"I'm not caught up in the initial infatuation. We're trying to decide if this is something solid. Besides, people tend not to want to stick around once you start unpacking your baggage."

"Z if I can be honest with you. You never let anyone in to really love you. You were with Sobray, but that wasn't love. I think you liked that he was emotionally unavailable. You didn't have to worry about really falling for him. I know y'all bonded because he was your first and only, but you didn't let him see the real you."

"How do you know? We didn't link back up until after."

"Yes, but I know you! I know what you told me about the relationship you had with him."

"Maybe you're right. I'm doing things different with Rohan. At least I'm trying to do things different with him. It's hard letting people in not knowing if they will stick around."

If only she knew how my relationship with my mom was haunting me. The suffocation of not knowing if she will stick around or if she's here to finish annihilating me.

"Yeah, yeah. Let me get you home so you can get ready, and I can start dinner for my pod at the house," Jilly rolled around on the park bench, trying to shift her weight so she could stand.

"Let me help you rollie pollie."

"I can't wait until this is you. It's going to be payback time!"

"That won't be no time soon, and by then, this moment will be the furthest thing from your mind," I assured her, taking her by the hand.

Jilly and I bounced around the names of my future goddaughter until I arrived in front of my apartment building.

I hurried upstairs so I could shower and get dressed to see my man. *My man.* It felt rewarding knowing I had a real man this time — someone who valued and respected me as a woman.

It's been three months and the only thing we've done is kiss. No sex. We both agreed to wait until we knew what this was. We decided that there was no point in creating sexual ties if we didn't have chemistry outside of the bedroom.

Best decision I've made in dating someone. Sobray still texts here and there. To my surprise, he hasn't crossed any lines or been disrespectful, but Sobray is known for playing the long game. He treats you like a queen until he knows he has you under his thumb. Once that happens, it's all downhill from there. Next thing you know you're getting slapped around and called out of her name.

I check his Facebook from time to time, and he has a new girlfriend now, so I'm confused as to why he still texts me. I keep it short and brief. Sometimes I don't respond at all because I don't want to give him the wrong idea or allow myself to fall for his charm. Besides, Rohan makes it hard to think of anyone else.

I was now a supervisor at my job, which came with a hefty pay increase. I put my furniture on layaway a piece at a time and paid it off so I wouldn't be in debt trying to do rent to own.

Once I had my house decorated and upgraded to my liking. I updated my wardrobe. It still wasn't anything expensive because that's just not me.

I found some affordable sexy pieces at some of the local stores in my neighborhood. I still shopped at thrift stores on the regular to save money.

I stuck to the financial advice Jilly gave me when I first moved in. My savings account is getting fat! I almost have two months' worth of my bills saved so far.

I was finally climbing out of the black hole I felt my life was being consumed in.

I ran my hands across my hips to straighten my white sleeveless dress. I wrapped a fuchsia scarf around my neck to accent my white and pink wedges.

Buzz! Buzz!

I pressed the button so I can let Rohan in. I know it was him because no one other than Jilly comes to visit.

I grabbed my purse and keys.

"Wow," Rohan exhaled.

He really boosts my self-esteem the way he acts like it's his first time seeing me with each encounter we have.

"Stop," I blushed, gently pushing him out the door so I could lock up.

"You are beautiful. You are blossoming right in front of my eyes. I'm in awe of your determination," Ro kissed me sweetly on the forehead.

"Thank you."

The ride to his place was filled with conversation about our day and work. Our poetry slams have been bringing the city out. Rohan was able to secure the building upstairs. The grand opening for that was coming up in a couple of months. He didn't bring my mother up, which was a plus.

"What is this?"

When I walked into his house, I greeted with red rose petals all over his black carpet. It was so soft it felt like velvet with your shoes off. Candles were placed strategically all over the living room waiting to be lit.

"I wanted to talk to you about something tonight," was the only response I got while he walked around lighting the candles.

"Okayyyy," I shifted nervously on the couch.

"It's not about earlier babe. I'll be right back," he said, disappearing out of the room.

When he returned, he had a bag labeled Pandora.

"I got this for you," he handed me the bag.

"You didn't have to do that."

"I know, but I wanted to."

I pulled the box out of the bag and opened it. It was a bracelet with a book and microphone charm dangling from it.

"The book represents our first encounter. It started crazy; I'm thankful for that moment. The mic is for the poetry slams that we started and now host together," Rohan was beaming with pride.

"Awweee, thanks babe!" I wrapped my arms around his neck.

"There's one more box."

My heart started to pound, and with each thump, I felt it leap further into my throat. I know we're nowhere near the point of me having to fear that a ring in this box but crazier things have happened.

My hand shook as I retrieved the box from the bag. Exhaling deeply, I opened it. It was a silver charm that read I love you with a small gold heart dangling from it. The card with it was inscribed with "*Love You Forever Collection.*"

I gasped, "Ro…I don't know what to say."

"We've been dating for three months now and I want to make it official. I want you to be mine. I hope you feel the same way. I understand if you don't want to say it back, but know that I love you."

Tears flowed from my eyes because for once a man had chosen me for all the right reasons. He took the time to realize the value I added to his life. Maybe my baggage wasn't scary to him.

"I do love you. I've known for awhile now that I had fallen in love with you, but I just wanted to make sure we were both on the same page. I would be honored to be your woman," I planted my lips on his and kissed him as if my life depended on it.

His hands explored my body and his touch was firm but gentle. His fingertips dug into my back as he laid his body on mine. The smell of Creed Aventus intoxicated my senses. I recognized it because I helped pick it out for him. I couldn't afford to pay the two-hundred and eleven dollars for it, but I was glad he wanted my opinion. I had made an excellent choice because I was dying for Ro to solidify our relationship in another way.

"We don't have to take it this far if you're not ready. I can wait as long as you need," Ro panted between kisses.

As if I could think straight or deny him after he'd laid out a scene from the perfect romance novel.

"I've never been so sure about giving my body to someone as much as I am about you. You're the second man that I've shared my body with. I'm not as experienced as what you're probably used to," I lowered my head in embarrassment.

He gently placed his hand on my chin and lifted my head, "You have nothing to be embarrassed about. Your inexperience honors me but it will be my pleasure to teach you while I please you."

That was it…that's all I needed. I was more than ready to give Rohan all of me tonight. He was more than worthy of my virtue.

"Okay."

He picked me up and carried me to his bedroom.

His mahogany wood four post bed was fit for a king. I sank into his sumptuous plum comforter. The rest of the night was filled with soul altering love making and endless orgasms. Honestly, I've never had an orgasm before tonight. I was hooked. Not on just how we connected when we made love, but how we were entwined continuously with one another not only physically but mentally.

Tonight, I became his and he was mine.

ROHAN

I watched Zora as she slept peacefully in my arms. She confessed to me that she was inexperienced, but she revived something in me that I thought was dead. Something that seemed lost when my fiancé broke off our wedding years ago. What I neglected to tell Zo was that it was my best friend Swade that she cheated on me with. A man I grew up with who lived next door to me until we graduated high school. After that, we attended the same college and pledged the same fraternity. I never saw it coming. I thought they were close because of my relationship with him. Boy was I wrong!

I not only felt love but hope with Zora. There's nothing I wouldn't do for this woman. I can't wait to see how we evolve together. Her issues with her mother don't bother me. I just need her to deal with it, so it doesn't contaminate what we're trying to build emotionally.

"Sleepyhead," I kissed her forehead and then her lips.

I knew she was exhausted since we devoured each other round after round. She was well worth the wait.

"What time is it?"

"It's seven. I didn't know if you had to work today, or maybe you wanted to go take care of the other thing."

"No, we're off this weekend, and I called to check on my mother. They're keeping her for a while until she's more stable. You can drop me off whenever you're ready."

"I'm in no rush unless you are."

"There's no other place I would rather me," she smiled.

"In that case, unless you want to sleep in, I would love to cook you breakfast."

"Let's sleep more; then we can eat."

"Or… I can eat, and then after I'm done feasting on you, then you can sleep," a devilish grin adorned my face.

I couldn't get enough of this woman.

"Well…have your way then," she stuck her tongue out with that wide smile of hers.

I wasted no time engulfing her. She was my first meal of the day.

As promised, when I was done, I allowed her to drift back off to sleep. I took a warm towel to my beard to clean her cream from my hair. After I was done, her scent still intoxicated me.

The rest of the day was spent with us just relaxing curled up with our books.

"I have family dinner later today. Would you like to join me? I would love for you to meet my family."

"Do you mind if I pass? I'm still a bit nervous about meeting them due to their perception of me stealing from you. I also have a lot on my mind concerning my mom."

"I understand but know that I got your back and I won't allow anyone to make you feel any type of way. You and my family are two of the most important things in my life. At some point, I will need you to meet them."

"I understand. I just want to enjoy us being in this bubble."

"Nothing wrong with that."

A couple of hours later, I dropped her off at home and headed to my parents for dinner. My heart was consumed with joy. Everything was finally lining up in my life.

I've invested some of the money from my settlement into the space above my bookstore. I was waiting for my liquor license to be approved and also my food permits.

Zora helped me nail down a limited but tasteful menu. I was happy about the grand opening coming up.

We've planned everything out and it was on track. All our contractors, vendors and wholesalers are all black-owned. Zora and I were adamant about keeping our black dollar in the black community by supporting other businesses.

My business, Zora, and I are becoming pinnacles in the community. It was something I'd strived for but never thought I would achieve.

When I think about it, I've checked off some primary goals since Zora came into my life. She was priceless and I will make sure I spend every day making sure she knew it.

I hopped out of the car once I pulled up to my parent's home. Everyone was already there but I didn't care; I was a bit late. Zora had me walking on air. I wanted to break out into a James Brown slide but I digressed.

"Hey baby!" My mother sang while embracing me. "You're late. Come sit down so we can start dinner."

"Why haven't you been on time lately?" Esdee pried.

"Mind your business," anger swelled up inside me.

"Aren't we in a mood today?"

"I'm actually in a great mood. You need to stay out of my business."

"We're always in your business baby brother," Deliana chimed in.

"Yeah, and that's the problem. I'm grown and I don't need y'all to micromanage me."

"I guess," Chalise said taking a sip of her glass of Chardonnay.

"It's a valid question son," my dad said. "We know things have picked up at the bookstore and your expanding. Is that the reason for your recent tardiness?"

"In part. For the past few months, I've been dating someone and we've just been engulfed with one another. I will be mindful of being prompt," I assured my dad.

"Dating someone huh?" Esdee rolled her eyes.

I imagine that LaDana had already mentioned to her that Zora and I are seeing each other.

"Yes."

"Well, who is she son?" My mother beamed with admiration.

"Zora is her name. She's been-"

"Wait…isn't that the girl who stole from you awhile back?" Esdee spat knowing she was aware of who Zora was thanks to her homegirl.

"Stole?" My mother's eyebrows wrinkled in confusion.

"It was a misunderstanding," I defended Zo.

"How you misunderstand you having to chase someone down the street for your property? You better not bring that thief around here!" Esdee continued her rant.

"First of all, you will not disrespect her on any level in my presence! I will not allow her to be verbally assaulted because you have a hidden agenda Esdee!"

"You going hard for someone you just met!" Esdee stare me down.

At this point, it was a standoff between her and me.

"You just mad I didn't want to smash your homegirl and indoctrinate her into this family. Respect my decision and stay out of my business. I'm a grown man!"

My dad nodded his head in approval for me, finally setting my sisters straight. Over the years, they have crossed so many lines. I allowed it because they've always protected me growing up.

They've been my armor and shield, but it was time that I am that for my lady. I needed to set the expectation before I brought Zora around them. She was already nervous about meeting them because of the mess LaDana told Esdee.

"Well, I can't wait to meet her son," my mother's bubbled with happiness.

To her, I was that much closer to marriage and having a baby. Deep down inside, I was hoping for the same. I would be lying if I said I didn't worry; at times I wondered was I making the same mistake I did with Nikia. I'm trying not to move so fast with Zora, but it just feels so right.

ZORA

I sat on the sofa sifting through my mail. I clenched my eyes and took a deep breath to calm me down. I've been taking some courses at Houston Community College. On a whim, I decided to apply for the Dental Assisting Program. I wouldn't be a full-blown dentist, but just to be in that field excited me. I loved teeth.

A conversation I had a while back with Rohan made me go for it. When he asked why I wasn't in school to be a dental hygienist, it triggered something in me. Maybe I was shrinking myself and thinking small.

I know I'm intelligent; I just never felt I could have an actual career that required a degree.

I pulled it together and opened the envelope.

"EEEEKKKK!!" I jumped up from the couch and danced around in the center of my living room. I got accepted into the program!

I can't wait to tell Rohan. He said he would call me once he was done with dinner. We were picking up where we left off earlier today with a movie night.

I was so excited I had to tell someone so I picked up my phone and called Jilly.

"Hello."

"Hey friend! Guess what?"

"What? Tell me!"

"I got into the dental assistant program at school!"

"You go girl! I told you that you would get in! I knew it!" She cheered.

"I know, right! Oh, let me send a picture of something else."

I put her on speaker while I snapped a picture of my bracelet Ro got me.

"Z, that's beautiful! I love Pandora. It's by far one of the most creative things Jared's has come up with. Wait…does one of those charms say I love you?"

"Yes. Rohan told me last night that he loved me!"

"Did you finally say it back?"

"Ummm."

"Z!"

"Girl yes! That's not all either."

"What else! What else girl?"

"We made love for the first time," I panted as I dropped my body down on the couch.

"Andddddd…how was it?"

My fingers trailed my chest, stopping between my cleavage.

"It was electrifying Jillian," I quivered.

"Girl, you used my government so I know there was some healing in that thing," she laughed so hard she started snorkeling.

"Shut up! On some real, he was a perfect gentleman. He even offered to wait if I wanted, but I want to make love to that man so bad I could taste him between both pairs of lips."

"Well look at you growing up."

"We bonded on so many levels last night intimately. I finally had an orgasm."

"Girl what?! You've never had one?"

"Nope. Never. Not until Rohan," warmth spread through me as thoughts of the night prior bombarded my mental.

Rohan had me howling with pleasure. It was as if I was caught up in this sensual rhapsody. I floated on every note he made me bellow and I wasn't sorry at all about it.

"Jilly, I have to go. I'm getting another call."

"No, you can't leave me hanging! We were getting to the good parts!" She whined.

"Girl, I'll call you back."

I clicked over and answered the call from the hospital.

"Hello."

"Ms. Mitchell?"

"This is her."

"Your mother is being released, can you come and get her? She will be ready in an hour or two," Dr. Bassin's disapproving tone let me know exactly what he thought of me not coming to see my mother.

"I thought she was being kept a bit longer for observation?"

"Well, she's stabilizing rather quickly and keeps asking to leave."

"I understand. I'm on my way."

I opened my app and requested an Uber. There was one in the area. My notification that my driver was outside arrived in about ten minutes.

My thoughts raced as I pulled up to the hospital. Was my mother okay to be home alone? Did I have to bring her home with me? Could I trust her at my house if she was there alone? I was busting my butt to get what little I did have in my apartment.

When I arrived, housekeeping was making their final rounds for the night. I maneuvered around their carts to get to the room number the lady at the nurse's station rattled off to me. I had only been on the hall a matter of seconds and the alarm on someone's monitor was annoying me.

The nurses huddled around the other nurse's phone to watch something on social media. They were in no rush to help the patient.

I wonder if my mom was ignored the same way. If so, was that the reason she wanted to leave. Or maybe she just wanted to get back to her drugs. Who knew?

"Hey mama, are you ready?"

"Yes. Let me go into the bathroom and get dressed," she dragged her body from the bed with her clothes in hand.

Her feet made a light scraping sound as her slippers made contact with the linoleum floors. The floors had a gloss on them from the recent wax.

"I have the paperwork that requires a signature for your mother to be released," the nurse explained.

"Can I sign it, or does she need to?"

"You can sign but I still need to explain her discharge instructions to her. She will need to sign off on those to confirm she understands."

"Okay."

My mother appeared from the bathroom. Her eyes illuminated her weariness. Drugs were taking a toll on my mother. I wonder if my questions about her past triggered her? I wonder if I was the reason she had fallen off of the wagon?

"I'm ready," she said.

"Mrs. Mitchell, I need to go over your discharge instructions with you. We also listed the information for a rehab program that Dr. Bassin said he could pull some strings to get you into when you're ready," she smiled.

"Okay," my mother was there physically, but mentally it didn't look as if she was.

The nurse went through the pages of paperwork, outlining what my mother could and couldn't do.

My phone started to vibrate. I checked it and it was Rohan.

My breaths quickened as I pondered if I should allow Ro into this part of my life. I could tell my mother's body was still weak, but she was just as stubborn as I was. I didn't want to have her waiting for an Uber with a stranger.

I sighed, rubbing the back of my neck, I decided to do what was best for my mom. I guess now would be as good a time as any to see if Ro could embrace all parts of my life.

I stepped out and answered the phone.

"Hello."

"Hey baby. What's wrong?"

"I'm at the hospital with my mom."

"I told you that I would go with you."

"I know, but I didn't want to interrupt dinner with your family."

"For this, you could've. This is important baby. Which hospital is she at again?"

"St. Mary's."

"Okay, what room?"

"They just discharged her so we'll be downstairs in the emergency waiting room."

"Okay, I'll be pulling up in about ten minutes. I have already headed towards your house anyway."

"Without calling me first?"

"You're my woman now. If I want to pop-up, know I will, and I did call you en route," he laughed.

I smiled from ear to ear. I loved that Rohan passionately pursued me.

"Is that so Mr. Jefferson?"

"Yes, it is Ms. Mitchell."

"Well, I guess that settles it. I will see you soon. I have to get back inside with my mother."

"Okay, I will call you when I'm outside."

"Okay love," I confirmed, disconnecting the call.

When I walked back into the room, the nurse was finishing up.

"C'mon mom. Our ride will be pulling up shortly."

"Okay."

"I'm sorry I didn't come earlier to check on you."

"I understand. You've had your share of seeing what my addiction can do to me. I was glad you didn't come. I couldn't stand to see the hurt in your eyes again knowing I keep disappointing you."

"Mom, did me asking you about your past trigger you to go on a binge?" I pressed the button to the elevator.

"Baby, I'm an addict. I'm in constant recovery until the day I die. Anything can trigger me if I'm not strong enough to fight my demons on any given day."

"What do you think about the rehab program Dr. Bassin said he could get you into?"

"That's one of the nice ones. I heard about it before but I never had the money to look into it."

"Let me help you. I can make some calls tomorrow and get the logistics and let you know what they say."

"I would love that," she smiled.

"Do you want to stay the night at my house?"

"No baby, thank you though. I want to get in my bed."

"If you need anything, can you please call or text me, mama?"

"I will baby. Thank you for helping me. It's more than I deserve."

"No, mama. You gave me life. I've been letting my bitterness from the past keep me stagnant long enough. As long as you help yourself, I will be there every step of the way. I won't allow you to sabotage my life though mama. If you start to spiral, I will cut you out of my life with no hesitation."

"That's fair," I helped her take a seat in the waiting room.

"My boyfriend is picking us up. He was adamant about meeting you mama," I waved enthusiastically at Ro who was coming through the automatic double doors.

"Oh, he's a fine one," she nudged me.

"I know right," I gripped her arm in agreement.

"Hello. Mrs. Mitchell, I presume?"

"Yes, nice to meet you," my mother extended her hand.

"Well, let me get you ladies in the car. It's getting late."

"Here mom, you sit in the front seat with Ro."

"Absolutely not! I'm okay to sit in the back. I'm sure the backseat will be more comfortable for me anyway," she insisted.

"Okay."

The drive home was pretty short. Shockingly, my mother lived only about two miles from me. Rohan helped me get her out of the car and settled in her apartment.

"Mrs. Mitchell, when you're up to it, I would love for you to come to have dinner with Zora and me."

My mother's caramel skin became flush with embarrassment. I know thoughts of the last time we tried to have dinner together was a disaster for us both.

I gently place my hands over hers, "I would love to try it again mama."

Her face relaxed in relief, "As soon as I'm up to it and we find out about the other thing, it's a date!"

"Well, I'll be sure to remind you. Don't forget to call me if you need anything," I reminded her.

"I won't."

We paused in the hallway until we heard her lock the top lock.

Once we were back in the car Rohan asked, "What's the other thing your mother mentioned?"

"I told her I would help her get into rehab."

"That's great! How do you feel about that?"

"Scared but hopeful. If it's possible to have her in my life, I want that for us both."

"You deserve that. So where are we sleeping tonight? My house or yours?"

"Let's do mine. I have to be at work in the morning so you can drop me off on the way."

"Cool, let me go by my house and grab an overnight bag."

We pulled up and there was a car sitting in front of his house with a huge red bow on it.

"Wow, somebody is going to wake-up in the morning with a sexy black Audi! No offense, but that one colder than yours," I teased him.

"Is that so," he smirked. "Can you come inside with me. I don't want you out here waiting alone."

"Let me find out you trying to get a quickie in!"

"Well, I wasn't, but since you brought it up…"

"Aht aht!" I slapped his hand from my thigh and opened the door.

Beep. Beep.

I looked strangely at the car parked in front of his house. I know they don't think anybody out here trying to steal.

Beep. Beep.

"Look ain't nobody trying to steal y'all lil' gift!" I yelled out to no one in particular.

I turned around to see Ro cracking up laughing. Literally on the verge of tears.

"What's so funny?"

"This is your car, Zora! I ordered it for you a couple of weeks ago. They called me shortly after I left my parents to let me know it was ready."

I just stood there, speechless. No one has ever done anything so beautiful for me.

"Well," he stood there waiting for me to respond, but my lips were paralyzed.

I could feel the warm tears against my sticky skin.

"I…I don't know what to say. Rohan, I can't accept this."

"You can and you will. Before I knew that you loved me back, this is something I wanted to do for you. I hate how much money you spend on Uber and public transportation if our schedules conflict. I hate you being in those cars alone with the strange Uber drivers. The title is in your name. You don't have to worry about any funny business if you wake up and decide you don't want me anymore. It's yours with no strings attached. Promise," he reached out his hand to hand me the keys.

"Thank you," I sobbed.

"Zora, I'm here to love you properly. That's it."

"I don't think I've ever experienced such a thing."

"Well, it's time to change that. So let me."

"Okay."

I took his hand and followed him inside. I just sat on the couch why he got his bag together stuck. I couldn't believe he did something like this for me. I was happy, but I was also freaked out.

If we don't work out, it would be devastating for me. Rohan has loved me like no other.

"I'm all set. I'll follow you in my car so we don't have to wake up early to drop me back off at home."

"Sounds like a plan."

"Don't be freaked out, Zo. This is how a man is supposed to love a woman he claims to love."

"I'm trying, but this is all new."

"Well, get used to it woman because you ain't seen nothing yet," he consumed my lips with his. My knees turned to water as passion snaked through my body."

His love was evolving me, in a good way as a woman.

ROHAN

Zora's car couldn't have arrived at a better time. She's been so focused on her other goals so intensely that I wanted to take this one off her plate. We spent the rest of the night making love. She pleaded for me to allow her to get some sleep so she could be on time for work.

I told her I could pay her to come work for me but she refused. She didn't want us to get tired of each other. She also tried to maintain her independence. I understood.

Now when I walked into my shop, I didn't feel the weight of the world on my shoulders. I felt accomplished now when my feet crossed the threshold.

The smell of cinnamon and maple flooded the air. Zo was into aromatherapy and I admit it added a little something extra to the ambiance.

"Good morning Mr. Jefferson," LaDana sang walking in with my coffee.

"Good morning. I told you that I don't need you to bring coffee over now that I have my machine."

"I know, but I've missed you. You have been so busy with your new friend. I rarely see you anymore."

"What are you talking about? I'm here all the time with Zo."

"Exactly," she rolled her eyes.

"Look LaDana; I want to be clear with you. Zora and I are officially dating. Matter of fact, I'm in love with that woman."

LaDana stood there with this blank look of hardness on her face. Somehow, I think she thought she still had a chance with me.

I've never led her on. I took her on one date. I knew for sure that we didn't vibe on the same frequency. Not like Zo and me.

"I guess congratulations are in order," she reached out to embrace me.

I initially hesitated but decided there was no harm.

"Well, I see some things never change," Zora said, standing at the door with my charger.

"Hi, Zima."

"You know my name, so stop playing with me," Zora snapped walking closer to LaDana.

"What Rohan sees in your ghetto self, I will never know."

"LaDana leave. Now!" I demanded her.

"Sure," she smiled devilishly. "Nice seeing you again Zena."

I grabbed Zora before she could get to Dana. I hated the way she let that girl get to her. I'm in love with her, not LaDana.

"I took an early lunch to bring your charger," she shoved it in my hand.

"Why are you making this a thing?"

"You know why I'm making this a thing! That heifer keeps chasing behind you and you enable her!"

"I just told her that I was in love with you, and she congratulated me."

"Yet she turns around and insults the woman you claim you told her that you love."

"Claim?"

"Are you calling me a liar? I warn you to tread carefully?"

"Or?"

"Or nothing. I won't be disrespected, Zora. I don't disrespect you, so don't insult me by insinuating that I'm a liar!"

I could feel my nose flare from the anger boiling inside me.

"You don't think it was disrespectful to be hugged up with her when I walked in?"

"It was harmless."

"What's up people?" Clayton interrupted our argument. "Sis, stop looking like an angry bear! Dang!" He nudged Zora, making her laugh.

"Boy, leave me alone! You get on my nerves," she showed all thirty-two which I was not feeling.

I don't know if she was doing this on purpose, but I wasn't feeling her interaction with Clayton at the moment.

"What can I do for you man?"

"Nothing, you know I check in with you before our day gets crazy. I didn't know your lady was here."

"It's cool. I was leaving anyway. I have to get back to work," she cut her eyes at me.

No, keep that same energy you had with Clayton with me woman. She was about to create a real problem if she didn't dial that friendliness back.

"Y'all good man?"

"Yeah, her and your sister just don't get along well."

"News flash! No one gets along with Dana!"

"All in all, things are good with us. I'm taking Zora to meet my family this weekend."

"I thought you said she was adamant about not meeting them?"

"Well, she doesn't have a choice. We're getting pretty serious, so I want her to start coming to our weekly family dinners."

"She mentioned a couple of times while she was over here doing inventory that they may not like her. She seems extremely nervous about it. She wouldn't go into it, but she said Dana told one of your sisters something about her."

"Y'all have been chatting it up when she's here doing inventory for me?" I folded my arms across my chest and stroked my beard.

"Yeah, she good people. I found out we both grew up in the same neighborhood, but our paths never crossed. She said she moved around a lot."

"Clayton, you cool and all, but don't be over-friendly with my woman. Just because we cool don't mean it's cool for you to be all in my woman's face. That's all me. I got her. Understand?"

"You know it ain't even like that. I would never violate you or your lady. Rohan, we've been boys since you opened this store. I have been a solid friend for you. I've shared my business knowledge and encouraged you on the way when you needed a sounding board. I thought we were better than this."

"We are but I'm not letting another snake come in behind my back and take my woman."

"Snake? Wooow! I'm going to let you have it today, Ro. I'll chalk this up to you having a bad day with your lady. I'm out," Clayton walked to the door shaking his head in disbelief.

I wasn't sorry. If I learned anything from Swade, it was to keep your woman close to you. I felt like Zora was different, but I wasn't taking the chance of putting her in any situations that could risk our relationship.

As a matter of fact, let me start making up.

"Hello, I would like to make an order," I said the lady on the other end of the phone at the florist shop.

"What can I get for you?"

"I would like three dozen long stem roses sent to the address on my account."

"Your name, sir?"

"Rohan Jefferson."

"We have two. One at an apartment complex and the other a business," she questioned.

"Send it to the business address on Rimrock please."

"What color roses would you like?"

"Aren't the colors the standard white, red, yellow, or pink?"

"We've culminated some hybrid colors, so we now have lavender, yellow with red trim and blue roses."

"Wow! Let's go with purple. That will give me a head start on getting out of the dog house with my lady."

She chuckled before confirming my order.

I couldn't wait for the call from Zora telling me how thoughtful I was. She could never stay mad at me long.

ZORA

"Look what I have," Sherica sang. "At least someone is appreciated by their man."

"Girl, he made me mad," I informed her rolling my eyes.

"Well, let's give him kudos for creativity. He sent purple roses girl. Purple! I've never seen purple roses. Have you?"

"No," I had to crack a smile because she was right. This was out of the box.

"Well, that man treats you like a queen, so I know it was something petty that made you mad," she whispered.

Sherica knew I made sure to keep these nosey women in this call center out of my business. I didn't tell Sherica to much, but I would say to her bits and pieces about Ro.

"Maybe you're right. I'll give him a call," I yielded.

I decided to wait until after work to call Rohan about the roses. I had to let him sweat a little so that he would know the severity of his actions.

I did love a man that made right his wrongs. I smiled as I caressed the petals of my roses. Perhaps I did overreact with Dana. Growing up in foster care, I was forced to fight and hold my own. It's the only way I know. It's how I survived this long.

I also hated showing weakness. That's exactly what was showcased every time I interacted with Dana. I won't keep falling for her scheme though.

As soon as I made sure my team was logged and clocked out, I made my way out of the building. I fumbled through my purse until I found my phone.

I had to set an example for my team, so I rarely had it out during work hours.

I had several messages from Ro to sum it up; he was anxious to know if I liked the flowers and if I accepted his apology.

"I will accept your apology if you accept mine," I immediately said once I heard him pick up.

"You know I do," he sang. "There is something I need from you," he continued.

"What's that?"

"I need you to come with me to meet my family tomorrow."

There was silence on the phone. He's been more than gracious with my mother and what she had going on. I can't be selfish. I need to face them if I planned to really be in Rohan's life. Regardless of their perception, it was up to me to change it and show them who Zora is.

"I would love to."

"Really?"

"Yes, I'm honored that you think enough of me to introduce me to your family officially."

"Thank you so much, Z! You don't know how much this means to me! I finally have a woman by my side that I can be proud of."

I beamed with pride. Rohan made me feel like the weight of who I am as a woman grounded him and made him stand taller as a man.

We complemented each other in all the right ways. I'm truly blessed. I never thought this would be my life. This is my winning season.

*　　*　　*

"Jilly! I desperately need you here!"

"I can't. I've been having complications with your god baby. I'm on bed rest boo," she whined. "EEEEELLLIIOOOOTTTT!" Jilly yelled in my ear for her husband. "Don't forget the Oreos or I'm going to forget you my husband, and punch you in the mouth honey bun!"

"Really?"

"Sorry for hollering in your ear but I need those cookies in my life. Now send me a picture of the options you have laid out on the bed. Better yet, put them on the wood floor so I don't have any other colors disrupting the flow of the fit."

"Okay, give me a sec."

I paired the outfits with shoes and accessories. I've been following a few fashion influencers on Instagram that have helped me come out of my shell of neutral colors. I was able to get ideas for affordable yet fashionable looks on YouTube.

"Okay, go with the light-colored denim jeans with the white wrap shirt. I like how the sleeves are puffed. Wear red pointed-toe shoes with the four-inch heel that I got for your birthday."

"I was going to wear white ones."

"No, the red will set it off. It'll give it a bit of a pop. Take a cute pair of slides and put them in your purse just in case y'all are there long. If you start to feel comfortable enough to kick your shoes off, you can still keep it classy."

"Right. Right."

"Okay, now your make-up should be flawless but do a natural beat. Use black eyeliner on the top and bottom of your eyelids so your eyes will pop. Your twist out is already flawless so no need to address that. Anything else?"

"I'm just extremely nervous, Jillian. What if they don't like me and Rohan breaks up with me or looks at me differently?"

"If he does, then that's his loss. If his family can change his perception or the way he feels about you without cause, then let him go. You're not going for their approval. You're going out of respect and love for your man."

"You know you cared if Elliot's family liked you or not."

"Yes, but I didn't need their approval. I love that we love each other, that's a bonus. You are always to respect his family, but he's already chosen you. You are there to show them why. That's all."

"Yeah, I hear you, but Rohan is big on family. I need this to go off without a hitch."

"I understand."

"Shoot!"

"What happened?"

"I need to get dressed. He's picking me up in an hour!"

"Okay, get dress and send me a picture of the finished product."

"Okay."

Steady Love was my song choice to set the mood as I got dressed. The song resonated with me and Rohan's love flawlessly.

We are two imperfect people with perfect love navigating through this thing called life.

I was ready in precisely an hour. I hurried and took a selfie in my full body mirror and sent it to Jilly.

She texted back a drooling emoticon. She sent back a drooling emoticon, which boosted my confidence even more.

"You look stunning," Rohan complimented me.

"Thank you. You know I had to match your fly."

His family lived in Sun Prairie, which was only a short drive to the diverse neighborhoods.

The houses were neatly spaced apart with perfectly manicured lawns. We pulled up in front of a yellow house with black trim. There was a wooden bench with yellow striped pillows with the words "love" and "family" written on them.

"Don't be nervous. I won't leave your side," Rohan held my hand firmly to assure me.

When we made it to the front door, Rohan just walked in. I guess it was his parent's house so it was appropriate.

Everyone was already in attendance. It would've been better if we were early, then I would be able to meet the members of his family as they arrived.

Chalise was the youngest and she was lovely. Her long hair danced on her shoulders and she had a smile that could light any room. Deliana was the middle sister and was giving me Bohemian vibes. She wore her hair natural in a twist out that she had colored to an Auburn color. Her deep chocolate skin was flawless. She appeared friendly as well.

"So you're the one who's been having my brother missing in action," a tall slender woman who resembled Sade approached me.

"Zora, this is my oldest sister Esdee," Rohan made the official introduction.

"Nice to meet you," I extended my hand but she just looked at it.

"Don't be rude Esdee," Ro spat.

"It's okay, Ro."

"Come and sit with me," Rohan's mother waved me over attempting to break the tension between the three of us.

The old me wanted to smack fire from Esdee. I wanted Rohan to see how much I've matured so I digressed.

I did as his mother asked and sat next to her on the couch.

"So tell me about yourself Zora."

I smiled bashfully, not sure really what to tell her.

"Well, I'm a supervisor at a call center. I enjoy helping Rohan out at the bookstore and reading a lot."

"Are you still trying to steal from him as well?" Esdee teased.

She was trying my patience. I knew this would come up at some point, but I didn't think it would be this early into the meet and greet.

"I was a different woman back then. It was a mistake I made that somehow worked out in my favor because I met Rohan," I smiled at him.

I could tell he was proud of the way I was handling his sister, but she had one more time and I was going to let her have it.

She was arrogant with this attitude that she was better than everyone else in the room.

"Esdee, you need to chill," Rohan demanded.

"It's not my fault you brought this hoodrat into our mother's home. Mama, you better count the china before she leaves after dinner," Esdee continued picking with me.

I'm a lot of things but I refused to be anyone's verbal punching bag.

"What is your problem with me?" I stepped to Esdee.

Rohan quickly got up from his seat to make some space between his sister and me.

"My problem is that my brother can do better than some project chick from the hood! I'm sure you'll be just like your junky mother!"

WAP!

WAP!

WAP!

I three pieced her so fast I caught the entire room off guard.

"Get this animal off of me," she screamed for her life.

"Zora get off of her," Rohan coached while pulling me off of his sister.

"You told them about my mother?"

"Z, it wasn't like that! I promise!"

"Take me home! Now!" I yelled.

I grabbed my shoes I'd kicked off and marched out of the door.

Before leaving out I turned to his mother, "I'm so sorry for disrespecting your house Mrs. Jefferson," I lowered my head and made my exit. I didn't wait for her to respond.

The ride home was silent between Ro and me. I couldn't believe he told them about my mother. So now they thought of me as a thief with a crackhead mother. I've never been so humiliated in my life. I've worked hard to evolve and enhance my life.

I wasn't going to let Rohan's family or anyone else take that from me.

"When I offered to pick you up from the hospital, Esdee was at the store with me. When she asked me what was wrong, I didn't think anything of it when I told her about your mom. I didn't know she would throw that in your face later."

"It wasn't her business in the first place."

"I know. That's my bad."

"I'm sorry about the way I acted. Please apologize to your mother again for me."

"I will, but Esdee deserved what she got. She was picking with you the moment she saw you. Sister or not, I'm not going to ask you to standby and be disrespected. You did what you have to and now she knows not to play with you."

I smiled. It made me feel good that he had my back.

ROHAN

Z called me a nervous wreck because Jilly was finally having the baby. It seemed like she's been pregnant for an eternity. It was funny seeing her wobble around with her petite frame. She was all baby too.

I agreed to drive Z because I didn't want her speeding through traffic. I've had to pay off two speeding tickets since she got that car.

Z was over at my house so much that there was no need for her to keep her apartment. I'm not sure how she will take it if I ask her to move in though. We've only been together six months and I don't want her to feel like I'm rushing her.

I couldn't hide the fact that I wanted her face to be the last and first thing I saw daily.

"Hurry baby," she whined.

"Z I'm going the speed limit. If I get pulled over it's only going to prolong us getting there."

She folded her arms across her chest while sucking her teeth.

I just ignored her. It was my fault she had become so spoiled and accustomed to having her way.

The navigator at the front desk of the hospital directed us to Jillian's room. When we walked in Elliot was beaming with pride.

"What's up man?" He asked.

"Nothing much. How are you feeling?"

"Jilly did all the heavy pushing. I was just the coach."

"I hear you. I can't wait until it's my turn."

"You hear that, Zora? Rohan is getting baby fever," he laughed.

"Well, let me find some Tylenol because ain't no babies coming this way," she sternly proclaimed.

"You're joking, right?"

"Ro, this is Jillian's moment. This is not about us right now," her eyes never left her god daughter's face.

"So, how have things been at the store?" Elliot asked breaking the tension in the room.

"Man, things have been great. We have the upper level open now so the business has been booming. Zora and I make a great team. I don't think there's anything we can't accomplish together."

She looked up and smiled at me.

"Do I hear wedding bells?" Jillian asked.

"Jilly don't be rude by putting them on the spot," Elliot exclaimed.

"It was a simple question."

"Jillian, if and when we arrive at that point, you will be one of the first to know," Zora chimed in.

"Aight bet," she laughed.

The conversations were light and random. The only thing I could think about was Zora saying she didn't want kids.

It wasn't like I wanted to knock her up tomorrow. However, I do need to know if she is totally against kids or she doesn't want them right now.

I hope she's so steadfast due to her working on her degree and not because of any other crazy reason.

I played nice until visiting hours were over. Seeing Zora with the baby did something to me. I imagined her holding our son or daughter that way. To observe the love she has piercing our baby's eyes, assuring them she would never leave their side.

Zora is naturally nurturing to all of those around her so it's driving me crazy that kids weren't in the picture for her.

I'm sure she had her reason, but they better be good.

ZORA

The ride home was filled with this awkward silence. Rohan was in the driver's seat pouting as if I dragged him to the ballet on the night of a playoff game.

We've only been together a hot six months and making a baby was not in the cards. I love the way he loves me down and treats me, but he could still switch up at any moment.

I was not bringing a baby in this world in no other circumstance but as someone's wife.

"Are we going to my apartment or your house?"

"I thought that I could drop you off at home. I'm exhausted. I had a long day and I want to sleep. We don't do much of that when we stay over at each other's house."

I gave him the side-eye and took a deep silent breath.

"Ro, the reason I'm not open to having kids is because of how I grew up. I know I would never choose drugs over my child but I'm still damaged. I'm terrified that there's a piece of my mother in me. I would destroy that kid like life tried to do me if there is," my tears revealed my heart's cry.

Rohan pulled in to a parking space at Monona Terrace. It was a beautiful place to sit at any time of the day. I was absolutely in love with this place.

"Get out."

"What?"

"Just get out, please."

I sighed but complied.

He took me by the hand and led me to the pier. We took a seat and I waited for him to explain why he brought me here.

"Zora, you're nothing like your mother. You're already nurturing and loyal to anyone you love. I've seen how that love has taken you to some dark places. Surviving has caused you to radiate with confidence, peace, and growth. I would never leave you to raise our child alone whether we're together or not. It's no pressure, but I desperately want children. I always have and I always will. I won't compromise that aspect of my life. I do need to know if not having children is a hard no for you."

"Thank you for your kind words. As of right now, I can't deny the way I feel. It may change but as of now…it's a hard no. Where does that leave us?"

"I'm not sure," he clasped his fingers, forming a pyramid.

We sat on the bench for another hour in silence while I tried to figure out if I had just lost the best thing that has happened to me.

I know what I said changes everything between Rohan and me.

The ride home was just as tumultuous as the previous one before our pitstop.

"Are you staying the night?" I asked when we pulled in front of my building.

"Not tonight," his response was as dry as Arizona in the summer.

"Well, call me when you make it home."

"Okay."

"I love you."

"Do you?"

I just looked at him in disbelief.

"So, the first time I say something you don't like my love is in question?"

"If that's what you want to call it. I have to get home, Z. I'll let you know when I make it."

"Don't bother," I said, slamming the door.

Fall was creeping in, so I pulled my sweater around me to block the cool breeze. It was nowhere near as cold as Rohan was tonight.

I should've expected something to go wrong. I don't know why I bother to get my hopes up.

I threw my purse down on the couch and followed behind it. I pulled my phone out and called Jilly. I needed to Facetime her to see my god baby. I was so in love with that little girl. I set a reminder on my phone to set my appointment for my Depo shot. I was thinking about switching my contraceptive due to all the good loving Rohan has been giving me. My hips are spreading, and my butt is barely squeezing in my jeans these days.

As mad as he is, I doubt I would be getting any loving any time soon.

"How did you know I would be still up? You know I just had a baby girl."

"Did they take her back to the nursery? I want to see her before I go to bed."

"You know this only girl is not going to this nursery. She's right here sleep on my chest," she flipped the camera view so I could see Tessa.

She was perfect. Her moon-shaped face adorned rosy cheeks. Her thick curly black hair made her look more Latino than African American. Her eyelashes were long and thick. If she weren't a baby you would think she had just got them done.

As Jilly breathe, her head lifted with the rhythm of her mother. If I had to guess, the sound of her mother's heartbeat was familiar and brought her peace in this new world she woke up in.

"Did you just call to stalk my daughter, or did you need to talk about what's bothering you?" Jillian interrupted me ingraining every inch of Tessa in my brain.

"I told Ro that I didn't want kids."

"How did he take it?"

"He reassured me I was nothing like my mother and assured me he would never leave me to raise our child alone when the day came for us to have one."

"You know that he's right Z. Right?"

"I know. I can't shake that nagging feeling in the pit of my stomach that says otherwise."

"At some point, you will have to figure out if Rohan is worth the comprise. If you can't see yourself living without this man then you will have to."

"I know. Look girl, you just had a baby. Get some rest. I will be by after work tomorrow to hold my G baby."

"Okay."

I ended the call and tried to find a way to get Rohan off of my mind. He never did text me that he made it home safe.

He doesn't get mad at me so I'm not sure how to take this. We've been vibing so well up until this point.

It still bothered me that he questioned my love. I rolled over to check my phone one more time before I drifted off to sleep — yet nothing from Rohan.

I pray we can get past this. I've become increasingly attached to Rohan. Not just because of what he does for me, but I love the way he loves me down. He's considerate and compassionate. If he sees a need in my life he handles it.

*   *   *

I sluggishly reached for the phone to disable the alarm. I was tossing and turning all night worrying about if this was the end of my man and me.

I sat up on the edge of my bed. I almost tripped over my shoes bolting towards the bathroom. I barely made it before vomit came spewing from my nostrils and mouth. It was utterly disgusting.

I must've eaten something that didn't agree with me. I pulled myself from the cold linoleum floors taking note that I needed to mop my floors.

I fumbled through clothes in my closet. I remember when I first moved in here, I only had a few outfits I rotated around. I still shop at the thrift stores but I have enough money now to go to the mall if I want.

School is getting ready to start, so being sick is not an option. I was determined to get my degree. Rohan lit up when I told him I got accepted. Since that man has come into my life, I swear that I've evolved into a better woman.

I looked at my phone and there still was no text or missed call.

I stuffed some crackers and a bottle of water in my bag. I grabbed my keys and headed out. I was usually at least forty-five minutes early but hovering over the toilet slowed me down a bit.

Pulling into the lot at work in my Audi made me feel like I was finally starting to live somewhat of a good life. Now, it only made me think of Ro. I still hadn't heard from him and it was starting to get to me.

I could no longer act like I didn't care if I saw him or not. I was utterly in love with this man. I need to find a way to get over my fears and come to a compromise.

After school, maybe then we could consider having a child together. That is contingent only on us being married. I know Ro to be a man of his word but I want a family unit, not a divided home.

"You look horrible!"Sherica didn't hold any punches with her slander.

"Wow. Thanks," I mumbled trying to make it to my office so I could log in and prepare for my day.

"What the?"

Before I could get my words out, I was diving for the trash can. I wasn't sure what I was hurling into the canister because I only was able to nibble on a couple of crackers on the way to work.

The smell of the donuts someone put on my desk to show their appreciation sent my stomach into a frenzy.

The warm aroma of sugar swirled into the air finding its way up my nostrils. Just the thought of it brought me to my knees.

The smell of my vomit made me hurl more. My body was becoming weak and I was sweating.

"Get those donuts out of here!" I yelled to Sherica.

She immediately grabbed the box and placed them on one of my employee's desk right outside of my office.

"I think I'm coming down with something," I panted pulling myself up from the floor.

"Yea, pregnancy!"

"Girl, I'm not pregnant. I have an IUD."

"You know how many people get pregnant on those?"

"Not a lot Sherica. I did my research before I got it put it."

"Well, I think you're in the small percentage that can still get pregnant on it."

"Whatever. Keep an eye on my team so I can go brush my teeth."

"You carry a toothbrush around?

"I'm in school to be a dental hygienist. Of course, I do. White teeth matter girl," I smiled heading toward the bathroom.

Once I made it back to my office I noticed a notification on my phone. It was Ro. He texted wanting to know if I was okay?

I smiled and admired the bond we're developing.

I texted him back that I was not feeling well but pressing through my day. I had classes later too and I refused to miss them.

By noon my nausea had settled so I decided to pick up a pregnancy test so I could use it later. I stuffed the box in my purse and stopped by Panera Bread on my way back to the office.

I wanted some soup and a light salad. I needed to get my strength back up. I had a full day ahead of me.

I guess Rohan was getting over himself. We've been texting back and forth all day. He even admitted to hating that he had to sleep without me next to him at night.

Up until recently, we rarely slept without each other. We took turns decided whose house we would spend the night at.

I've been so consumed today that I failed to check on Jilly and Tessa.

My stomach was in knots at the thought of having a bundle of joy resting on my chest. A smiled at the fact that I could become someone's mother.

The rest of the day was a blur. The only thing I could think about was the pregnancy test in my purse that seemed to weigh a ton.

I dropped my bookbag when I made it to my apartment and pulled the test out of my purse. I had been forcing water down my throat all day so I could do my business when it was time.

I removed the stick from the package and placed it between my legs into the flow of my urine.

I replaced the cap and wiped myself. I paced the floor, waiting for the word to pop-up that will change my life forever.

"What?"

My heart dropped when I read the words, "Not Pregnant."

That couldn't be right. Could it?

I don't know why I let Sherica get me all excited. I knew I wasn't pregnant. I told her it was just a bug. Wait until I get to work in the morning.

I'm glad I didn't jump the gun and get Rohan's hopes up with mine.

Just as I was getting into the shower, I heard a knock on the door.

"Who is it?"

"Sobray."

I stopped in my tracks, pausing with my hand on the doorknob.

What could he possibly want?

I reluctantly opened the door. Sobray and I don't have the best history. He tried to repair it a while back but Rohan blocked all of that action.

"I'm sorry to pop up at your crib, but I didn't have your new number."

I just stood there waiting for him to get the point of why he was at my house unannounced.

"I know you're wondering what I'm doing here. My mama died Z," tears appeared out of nowhere flowing from his eyes.

His mama is his heart, so I know he's hurting. He knew she and I were close so I was thankful he told me.

She helped me through my miscarriage. I tried to curl up and die with my baby. She didn't allow that to happen though.

Every day she forced me to start back living.

"I'm sorry to hear that. Are you okay?"

"I'm hanging in there. I just wanted to let you know that her funeral is this weekend. I really would like you to be there."

"You know I will be there."

"Thank you, Z. You look so different. You're glowing."

"Thank you. I had to do a lot of internal work on myself. Slowly I'm starting to evolve into someone I can be proud of."

"That's dope. I'm glad to see your doing better. The services will be at her church at eleven in the morning on Saturday."

"Okay. If you need anything for the funeral please let me know. Against my better judgment, I put my number in his phone. I prayed he would only use it for his mother's funeral. I didn't need any unnecessary drama in my relationship over an old boyfriend."

"Thanks again, Zora," Sobray smiled and embraced me.

"What's going on here?"

My mouth dropped open when I saw Rohan towering over us.

"Sobray stopped by to tell me that his mother passed," I explained.

"Sorry for your loss man," Rohan said.

"Thanks, man. I meant no disrespect. Zora and my mother were close. I didn't have her number so I took my chances and stopped by."

"No worries, man. I trust her. You keep your head up man," Rohan extended his hand and pulled Sobray into an embrace.

This man keeps giving me reasons to fall in love with him all over again.

Sobray excused himself, and Ro walked in and closed the door behind him.

"Are you okay?"

"Yeah. When I didn't have a place to stay his mom took me in. She made sure I had clothes and fed me. She was like a mother to me when she wasn't high."

"I was talking about earlier when you said you've been sick all day."

"Oh, yes I'm okay now."

I didn't bother to tell him I thought I was pregnant because he didn't talk to me for a full day almost when we couldn't agree on having a baby.

"Zora, I apologize for my actions the other night. I was a brat when I couldn't get my way. It wasn't fair to question your love. I'm honored that God has chosen me to be a witness of your process and evolution to greatness."

Rohan was transforming me into a softy. I couldn't hold back the tears that his words caused to manifest. My heart was full. My past had just left, and there was no residue of the pain I endured or the toxic love I couldn't shake. My future was standing before me and I embrace it fully.

"Ro I would love to start a family with you one day, but it will be as your wife and not your girlfriend. Our child deserves a unit and that's what we'll give them. I was scared at first but you're right. I'm not my mother. I survived everything meant to break me and I'm a better woman for it today. Thank you for loving me properly and helping me to recognize my worth."

"You ready to make-up?" He asked swooping me into his arms and heading to my bedroom.

*   *   *

"Oh God!"

I almost fell and broke my neck bolting to the bathroom. Once again, I was praying to that porcelain god in my bathroom. If I wasn't pregnant I needed to find out why I was sick for the second day in a row.

"You okay baby?"

"Yeah, I've been waking up sick to my stomach the past couple of days."

"Are you pregnant?"

"No, baby. I took a test and you know I have the IUD in."

"Those tests are not God. Make an appointment with your doctor and let me know when to be there," he demanded.

"Okay baby," I conceded.

Ro helped me from the floor so I could get cleaned up. When I got out of the shower he already had my clothes out for the day.

"Baby, you should call in."

"Ro, don't start. You know I hate missing work. I've never missed a day in the last couple of years and I'm not about to start. If I start to feel worse, I promise I will leave early though."

"Okay," he pouted.

It was cute because he was this tall buff man who was nothing but a big teddy bear when it came down to it. I loved it!

I did as he instructed and called my doctor. Because of my history of a previous miscarriage, she made me come in the same day. I called Ro and told him I would go on my lunch break to see her.

He insisted on picking me up.

Ro reached over and covered my hands with his. I was wringing them until they had started to turn red; I was so nervous.

"It's going to be okay. Whatever it is, we will figure it out. As you said, it could only be a bug or something," tried to reassure me.

We got in and walked directly to the back. I had explained before coming in that I would be on my lunch break. She had me take another urine test and she also had blood drawn.

Ro and I sat in the room waiting for the results of the urine test, which I already knew would be negative. If anything, we had to wait for the results from the blood work.

My doctor walked back in holding her clipboard, "Congratulations! You're pregnant!"

"What? How? But the test said-"

"Those tests are not doctors. It gave you a false negative. I know you're on your lunch break, but I need you to make another appointment so we can give you a full work-up."

"Okay."

"Look, I'm going to take good care of you," she assured me.

I looked over at Ro who was smiling from ear to ear with his water head. Lord, is my baby going to have his big head?

"I knew it!" He screamed once we got out of the doctor's office showering me with kisses.

"I have one request," I told him.

"Anything!"

"Can we not tell anyone until I'm in my second trimester? I had a miscarriage before and I don't want to jinx anything."

"I'm sorry baby. Is that another reason you didn't want to have kids again?"

"Yes."

"Anything for you. This will be our blessing. Once you're ready, we can tell people."

"Thank you."

"Having my baby. What a lovely way of saying how much you love me. Having my baby, what a lovely way of saying what you're thinking of me. I can see it your face is glowing," Rohan sang at the top of his lungs in the car off-key.

He was slaughtering *Paul Anka's* song, but it made my heart smile.

It wasn't like I'd plan, but I was grateful for my blessing. God was restoring everything I lost in my past. I was genuinely thankful that it was now my time.

ROHAN

No lie, I played it off, but I was livid when I popped up on Zora and saw that jerk she once dated before me. The way she flew off the handle when she walked in and saw me hugging LaDana, you would think she would be above this.

Once I found out she was pregnant with my unborn child, my anger subsided. All I could think of was how amazing we're going to be as parents.

Our child wouldn't want for anything. I will have him or her reading before their out of diapers. Just watch.

I was overflowing with joy.

I never told a soul, but Nikia was pregnant with my child. She selfishly aborted it without telling me. The only reason I found it is because I had to rush her to the hospital because she was hemorrhaging after.

Zora was giving me back everything that was taken from me without knowing. For that authentic show of love, I will die trying to give this woman the world.

"Baby, do you need me to pick you up from work?"

"Ro, don't start!" She scolded me.

"What I do?"

"Don't start to coddle me! I'm pregnant, not disabled!"

I rolled my eyes while she threw her tantrum. Little did she know that I planned on spoiling her and getting on her nerves thoroughly.

"Babe, you know I drove to work today anyway," she laughed.

If I had my way, her feet wouldn't touch the ground. I would carry her anywhere she needed to go.

"I guess lil' girl," I teased, returning the laughter.

Zora and I laugh more than we fight or argue. That was something rare in this era. Everyone feels they're right in their own eyes and not bashful to tell you about yourself.

I didn't talk to Zora when I found out she didn't want kids because I had to search within myself to see if I could find peace with her decision.

If she never changed her mind, would I be okay with not seeing a part of me walking this earth?

Once I had concluded, she had decided to stretch her convictions for me. I wouldn't disappoint her either.

My ultimate goal is to make that woman my wife.

I pulled in front of my bookstore. The business has been so fantastic that I've been able to hire staff to help me run the place.

I was becoming kind of a big deal in the city of Madison and I loved it.

It's finally my time, after feeling like I've been pushed to the back of the line time after time.

"You're chipper today," LaDana was outside clearing a mess customers had left behind.

A few empty coffee cups and half-eaten cakes were all that remained of a sloppy patron.

"I'm alive. I have a woman who loves me, and business is booming!" I sang.

I ignored the way LaDana's face twitched when I mentioned Zora. I didn't care. I would continuously lift her until Dana got the picture that Zora wasn't going anywhere.

"I guess. Enjoy it while it lasts. You know things are only good in life for so long," her sarcasm struck a nerve.

Deep down, I'd been trying to circumcise those exact thoughts from my mind.

ZORA

The past thirty days have flown by. Various emotions were consuming me like a tsunami. I was most grateful for another chance to become a mother again. As much as losing my baby almost caused me to die with it, I know now that I wasn't prepared to be a mother back then.

Now, I have my place, job, and car. I'm pursuing my degree to position myself to make even more money doing something I love.

I don't doubt that I can count on Rohan to be an amazing father, but I'm going to always make sure I can hold my child down. If he wakes up one day and decides he wants nothing to do with us, I will be prepared.

I've been running like crazy trying to help my mom with her sobriety. I was on my way now to take her to a meeting. She stuck with her inpatient treatment so now she was in an outpatient program.

Most of the time she caught the bus, but lately, she had been complaining of not feeling safe at the bus stop and on the bus.

"Baby, I told you I could take the bus today," my mom huffed, pulling herself into my car.

My mom was a slender woman, but the years of smoking had taken a toll on her lungs. She was winded trying to get into the car.

Having my mother in my life was just another testament to the hand of God restoring me piece by piece.

"Mom, you said you didn't feel safe and I agree. I saw a video on Facebook the other day that had me livid! I don't know who's raising these juvenile delinquents but I'm not confident in our future," I complained.

"I know the feeling. Your face looks fatter and you're glowing," her gaze was fixed on me waiting for a response.

"You know I've been watching what I eat and working out."

"Uh-hum."

I was relieved my mother didn't pry. I imagined she didn't want to make waves being that we're just getting back on solid ground.

"How have you been feeling?" I asked her.

"I've been well. Taking it one day at a time. How are you and Rohan doing?"

"We're doing well mama."

"Make sure you don't run him off. He seems like a good man Zora."

"Excuse me?"

"I wasn't trying to offend you baby, but you know you are stuck in your ways sometimes. Some men don't like an obstinate woman," she warned me.

"Mama we ain't back in the sixties. Women have a voice now. We didn't leave the slave masters house to become slaves to our men. Some women do have their own minds. I mean we're birthing babies and running boardrooms."

"Calm down girl. I must've pushed a button?"

"No, you didn't. I hate when people imply that a woman's only job is to listen to her man."

"I never said that Zora. You just took it that way. All I was trying to say is that a successful relationship takes compromise from both people. Don't forget; I have to stop by the hospital and do this blood work before my meeting."

"I know mama."

"Ms. Mitchell, you can go upstairs to the third floor now that you've signed in."

"Okay, thank you," my mother replied to the front desk receptionist.

I've never really liked hospitals. They're always unusually cold. I understand it's an attempt to kill germs but it was still creepy.

I tried to allow my reasoning to loosen the knots in my stomach.

"What are you doing here?"

My mother was frozen in her tracks as she stood face to face with an unfamiliar man.

His chiseled square jawline accented his deep-set eyes and thick eyebrows. His tight eyes made him look sneaky and mysterious. His salt and pepper hair was tapered and adorned natural curls.

"My daughter just had my first grandchild. What are you doing here?"

"None of your business."

"Oh, none of my business but you can be all up in mine," he snapped back.

"Mama, who is this?" I finally interrupted.

The man's eyes locked with mine and his widened. He looked at my mother and then back at me.

"You didn't."

"What was I supposed to do? Knock on your front door and tell your wife I was pregnant with your daughter as well?"

"Wait. What?" I said. "You told me you didn't know who my father was?"

"Is that what you told her?"

My mom had this dumbfounded look on her face as all of her skeletons came pouring out of the closet.

"I had a right to know!" He spat through clenched teeth.

"You rather allow me to be passed around in foster care than to tell my father I existed?"

"Foster care?"

"Yeah. She was high out of her mind and I burned myself trying to remove a pot from the stove. I didn't know I had third-degree burns until the nurse called the paramedics to my school," I raised my sleeve to show the man I now knew to be my father.

"I can't do this," my mom clutched her purse and bolted through the door labeled stairs.

I was standing there with this stranger not sure precisely what to say.

"I never knew about you," he finally spoke up.

"Same."

Despite him being my father, I still didn't feel comfortable bearing my soul to him.

"Can I give you my card? Whenever you're ready, I would love to talk to you and get to know you. I wish I would've known."

"What about your wife?"

I noticed him flinch.

"She passed a couple of years ago."

"I'm sorry to hear that but I'm sure your other daughter won't be jumping for joy to find out you have a daughter coming out of the woodworks."

"I told my wife a long time ago about my affair with your mother. My daughter is aware of it as well. I made a mistake a long time ago, but you weren't one of them. Forgive me, but what is your name?"

"Zora. My name is Zora."

"Really?" He grinned, his teeth glinted white against his chocolate skin.

"What?"

"Your mother and I met at a bookstore fighting over a book by Zora Neil Hurston," he informed me.

"Oh."

On the outside, I acted nonchalantly, but internally all I could think of was how Ro and I finally clashed in the bookstore.

"Well, I won't hold you hostage. You have my information when you're ready."

I watched him disappear around the corner. I was guessing he was headed back to my sister. Sister? I have a sister. I wondered if there were more of us. I'd be alone for so long but now my life is filling with more people than I ever could imagine to love me.

"That was your grandpa baby," I rubbed my slightly protruding stomach.

I marched off to find my mother. There was no way I was taking the stairs so I took the elevator back down to the lobby.

I was livid at my mother but I couldn't afford for her to fall off of the wagon so I had to be gentle with her.

Who keeps a child from their father? I don't care what the situation is; some things are beyond reproach.

"Here you are," I spoke through gritted teeth.

"I thought I could raise you on my own without him. I was doing okay until the crack epidemic hit the streets. Just one night of feeling I deserved to let my hair down and be irresponsible caused me to lose everything that mattered to me," she sobbed.

"What you did was messed up and I'm not letting you off easy, but I need you to get upstairs to that meeting."

She nodded in agreement.

"I'll wait for you down here. I don't feel like going back upstairs."

"He's a good guy. It was my decision not to tell him about you," she said turning to head back to the elevators.

I ignored the cramps tearing through my abdomen. I figured it was due to me not eating all day. I need to remember that I'm eating for two now.

I had time to run out and grab something. I would be back in plenty of time before my mom was done.

I pulled out of the parking garage. I was craving Jamaican. There was this quaint restaurant in Monona that served authentic jerk chicken with rice and peas.

SKKKRRRTTTT! BAM!

ROHAN

I no longer felt despair when I pulled up to my bookstore. Since the expansion, I was able to hire staff to run everything.

LaDana was on the porch next door, cleaning up the mess lazy coffee patrons left behind. She tossed the empty coffee cups and used napkins in the trash.

She occasionally still hinted that there could be hope for us but I just ignored her. I quickly countered her suggested with accolades about Zora.

"Look who decided to join the rest of us working folks," she crossed her arms as she teased me.

"Girl, I been working before you even woke up to start your day."

"What are you cheesing about?"

"Life."

"What about life?"

"I'm just thankful. My business is booming; I have a woman I adore that makes me better, and I finally found some peace in my life."

"Well, enjoy it while it lasts," I saw her mouth twist sarcastically.

"Why must we as black people go out our way to pull each other down? As soon as one of us starts to ascend we pull out our bow and arrows and shoot them down. I'm not going to let your bitterness disrupt my joy or my day," I left her standing there with her mouth open.

I lit into LaDana because secretly, she pulled out a nagging feeling I've been trying to override. This was also her second time making a similar statement. It was as if she was waiting for things with Zora and me to fall apart.

In the back of my mind, I was thinking that my life was starting to feel too good to be true. When things would come together, they would dissipate just as quick.

My vibrating phone forced me to loosen my grip on it.

"Hello."

The woman on the other end was rambling something about Zora getting into an accident. I didn't catch the voice until the end of the call to understand it was Zora's mother.

I felt a clutch up panic in the pit of my stomach. Something was wrong and I could tell.

I was literally at the hospital in about seven minutes.

"I'm here for Zora Mitchell," I yelled at the registration clerk on the other side of the emergency room glass window.

"Sir, please calm down."

"Don't tell me to calm down! Where is my fiancé?" I demanded.

"Go through the double doors. They had to rush her into surgery but her mother is in the waiting room already."

When I walked into the waiting room, Zora's mother was there with eyes swollen shut from crying.

"This is all my fault."

"What happened?"

"She was waiting for me to get out of my meeting. I didn't know she left. I got turned around trying to find my way out through the back when I didn't see her in the lobby. Somehow I ended up in the ambulance port. I lost it when I saw them pull Zora out the back. There was so much blood," she said, resting her head against my shoulder.

I held her as I silently prayed for the safety of Zora and my unborn child.

After a few hours had elapsed, I was done waiting. I needed answers.

I walked with purpose and intent back to the nurse's station.

"Is there word on the condition on Zora Mitchell?"

"If you would go back to the waiting room the doctor will be done as soon as he has her stabilized."

"Stabilized?"

"Please, sir," her dismissive tone made me want to snatch her over the counter.

"Rohan," Zora's mother called out to me.

When I turned around, the doctor was coming out. He pulled his mask from his face so he could bring us up to speed.

"Are you the family of Zora Mitchell?"

"Yes," her mother and I responded in unison.

"She's stable but she lost the baby."

"Baby?" Her mother looked at me in confusion.

"She was waiting to tell anyone until she got out of her first trimester. She was terrified of miscarrying again."

"Again?"

I wasn't in the mood to bring her up to speed so I ignored her questions.

I was starting to feel despair in every part of my body, not only for me but for my Zora. I don't know if she could survive another miscarriage even if it weren't due to her body betraying her this time.

I also grieved for my unborn child. This would be me and Zora's second loss of a child. Maybe she was right. Perhaps we shouldn't try this again.

"When can we see her?"

"Give us another hour. We're waiting for her to come completely from under the anesthesia. She's going to be extremely tired."

"Does she know about the baby?"

"No. Before we put her under that's all she kept asking. I felt it would best to come from one of you."

"I can't disappoint her again today," her mother quickly bailed.

I didn't expect her to tell Z about our baby but she didn't even let the idea marinate out there before jumping ship.

I understood, though. Her and Zora's relationship is rocky at best.

My body felt as if it was floating as I tried to formulate words to tell my baby that we lost our baby.

ZORA

Every bone and joint in my body cried out in agony as I came to. The last thing I remember is a truck running a traffic light and crashing into the side of my car.

"What's wrong?" I asked Rohan whose hand was wrapped so tightly around mine; I couldn't move it.

"How are you feeling, baby?" He countered.

"Stop stalling. How is my baby?"

He was eerily silent, which told me all I needed to know.

"I lost the baby, didn't I?"

I could feel every nerve in my body cry out in sorrow.

I snatched my hand from Rohan.

"Z?" My name broke from his lips.

I know he was hurting too, but I was the one who had started to feel my child move inside of me. I was the one with the morning sickness and mood swings. I was devastated.

"Do you know when they're releasing me?" I asked him.

"No, but I'll go and check for you," sadness flickered in his eyes.

This has been a horrific day. First, I find out about my father and then I lose my baby all in a matter of hours.

My gaze fell on my swollen hand. The IV must have slipped out of the vein because my hand was puffy. I didn't care. I was back numb to life. I keep allowing myself to think my life would be different, but it never is.

It's consistently filled with misfortune and disappointments. I was over it all.!

Rohan reappeared and I was hoping it was to tell me I was going home.

"The doctor said he would be in shortly but he's keeping you for at least forty-eight hours Zora."

"Are you kidding me? I have to get to work and school!" I spazzed out.

"Z, you just got into a major accident that caused your body extensive internal trauma."

"I've lost a baby. The trauma is not that extensive!"

I watched Rohan's eyes darken with pain. I hated what I was doing to him; I couldn't stop myself from spiraling out of control. Someone had to pay for my pain.

"Baby, that's uncalled for," my mother spoke up.

"This is your fault! If you were taking care of your own business instead of dragging me down with you, I would've been at work and still pregnant!"

My mother burst into tears clambering for the door.

I could see Jilly on her way in as my mother ran out.

"Is everything okay?" She asked.

Usually, I would be overjoyed to see my goddaughter but today she was just a reminder of what I lost.

"What do you think?" I snarled.

She cut her eyes to Rohan who just shook his head and took a seat in the corner.

"Well, I brought someone to help cheer you up," she smiled earnestly.

I could feel my body tense with tension, "Why would you think to bring a baby you didn't even want to see me after I lost mine would cheer me up?"

"I know you're hurting so I'm going to let that slide! Since we've been together, I've been by your side through whatever. That's not about to change. Stop pushing us away Zo! Let us help you through this," her eyes pleaded with me even more than her lips.

I could read the words that she couldn't express with Rohan in the room. She was begging me not to shut down and self-destruct.

I wanted to hear her. I tried to stop myself from going over the edge, but I just couldn't. I was tired of the pain.

I've been fighting tooth and nail to become the best version of myself only for my progress to be thwarted.

I wasn't sure how I would process this but I didn't want anyone else to get hurt with me.

At that moment, I thought of my dad. How he was by my sister's side while she gave birth to her child, but here I was mourning the death of my child. Where was he? Where was my support and love for my father? My mother was so selfish; I doubt if she even tried to tell him what happened.

If she had told him I probably would only lash out at him too. I just met the man today. It wasn't realistic for me to expect him to be here for me.

"Zora?" Jilly called out to me, jolting my mind back into the room.

"I hear you. I'm tired. I want to rest now," I turned my back to her and Rohan.

I wasn't tired; I couldn't face them at the moment.

"Baby, I'm going to the house to pick up some of our things," I heard Rohan say.

I didn't respond, hoping he would just leave me be. He did, and so did Jilly.

I could hear Rohan help her out the room, and I was glad to be alone finally.

I curled into a ball and cried as I clutched my hand to my heart. It was a failed attempt to keep it from feeling as if it were being ripped from my chest.

ROHAN

I couldn't stop the tears from falling from my eyes on my way to the bookstore. I wanted to make sure they locked up properly. There were a couple of times that Patrick, my store manager, forgot to set the alarm. He is a good kid with a lot of potential, so I worked with him.

I threw my head back in frustration. I don't know why LaDana was still working next door this late, but hopefully, she wouldn't notice me sneak in to check my alarm in the bookstore.

I did my best to dry my eyes to avoid any awkward conversations. I really didn't want Dana catching my wrath for something that wasn't her fault.

I hopped out of my car, careful not to slam the door. I unlocked my door and quickly went over to the keypad. The alarm didn't beep once I entered, so I knew Patrick forgot to set it.

"Why are you sneaking in here like a black ninja? If I hadn't seen your car, I was about to start shooting in here," she joked.

"Oh, Patrick forgot to set the alarm. I was stopping by right quick to check on things," I avoided eye contact.

"Are you okay Ro?"

"Yeah, I'm cool," I lied.

"You don't look cool. You like you're barely holding it together."

"I'm fine Dana," I reiterated.

"Ro," her eyes blazed with compassion.

A sob rose in my throat, "She lost the baby."

My head moved drowsily against her shoulder as she held me. The tears were flowing like a busted pipe.

I knew Dana was the last person I should be falling apart with, but I was full.

Attempting to be strong for Z while enduring her harsh words broke me today. I was hurting too. I lost another baby also! I was sick to my stomach.

Dana's small frame started to collapse under the weight of my agony. I stood up and gathered myself.

"Sit and talk to me. You can't go back to her in this condition. You need to get this out. We were friends long before our lives headed in different directions."

I was hesitant but she was right. I needed someone to talk to.

"Zora got into a car accident today. No one knew, but she was pregnant. She wanted to make it out of her first trimester."

"I had no idea. I'm so sorry about my sarcastic comment earlier. I feel terrible."

"It's not your fault. It's the jerk who ran the light fault."

"Well, I know you have to go but I'm here if you need to talk."

"Thanks Dana," I embraced her.

I usually wouldn't allow her to hold on as long, but tonight I appreciated her being there for me.

I needed to get that off of me so I can be in the best headspace for Z.

*   *   *

TWO DAYS LATER.   I was growing tired rather quickly of Zora's rudeness. I was always apologizing to the nurses and doctors for her attitude. They all were so understanding due to our loss but it still gave her no right to treat people the way she did.

The loss of our child shook the foundation of our relationship. I wasn't sure where this left us. I didn't feel any different about Zora, but I could tell she felt different.

I know she needed space so I didn't object when she said she wanted to go home and be alone.

"Do you want me to drop your pain pills off to you once they're done?"

"Yes, I need to pick up my rental until my car is fixed. I spoke with my car insurance agent, and I have to go to Enterprise."

"You don't think you're jumping back into things to fast Z?"

"I can't put my life on hold forever Ro. I can't miss to many days of class and the same goes with work. I have to push past this."

"I understand. Whatever you feel you need to do just make sure you heal properly Zora."

"There's no point of healing. I only get torn apart later. For now I'll settle for getting through the moment," she closed the door to her room behind her.

I took it as my que to leave. If she wanted me she knew how to get in contact with me when she was ready.

ZORA

I called Ro bright and early the next morning to come and pick me up. There was no way I was waiting around all day for him to take me to get my rental.

He felt I should take it easy but there was no need to. It wasn't like I was still pregnant. I pushed the pain to the back of my mind and kept it moving.

I was already waiting in the parking lot when he pulled up.

"You know I would've come upstairs to get you."

"I know but I need to take care of some business. I have a meeting at my school to see what all I need to turn in to catch up."

"I understand."

I kept my conversations with Zora real short these days. She had one more time to spew her venom and I would be relentless about getting my point across to her.

Once I took her to her rental I was going over to my parents' house.

"I need to stop by the shop on the way to Enterprise."

"You can't do that after?"

"Look, you're not the only one who has stuff to take care of today. I've been patient about your stank attitude lately but don't push it woman!"

She squirmed in her seat but didn't snap back.

"I might as well get me some coffee while I'm here," she rolled her eyes.

"Might as well," I huffed.

"I'm surprised to see you out and about so soon," LaDana stopped Zora in her tracks.

"Why so?"

"Rohan told me about the accident and the miscarriage."

If looks could kill I would be six feet under. My spine stiffened as Dana's words rolled off the tip of her tongue.

"He did what?"

"Baby I-"

"Don't baby me! Take me home!"

"But-"

"Now Rohan Jefferson!" She screamed causing those in the vicinity to stare.

Once we were in the car she lit into me like a piñata.

"You know she can't stand me and you tell her about one of the most devastating moments of my life! You couldn't wait to tell this trick my business. What else did she offer you to cry on?"

As insulted as I was I knew now was not the time to defend myself or feed into her anger.

I was wrong so I had to eat this loss like a man.

"It was innocent. I stopped by the shop to make sure the alarm was set after we found out you lost the baby. She was outside cleaning and noticed my demeanor. I was trying to be strong for you but I broke down when I least expected it."

"Tuh," she smacked her lips. "You know what. This time was the last time you make me feel some type of way about your plan b that works next door. I'm done with you Rohan," she didn't give me a chance to respond before hopping out of the car.

I slid out of the driver's seat to run after her.

"What do you mean we're done?"

"You're an intelligent man. I said what I said," she snatched her arm from me.

I was mortified by her words. Did she really mean them? She walked away from me as if she meant what she said.

I was confused. I made a mistake but not one that should've ended us.

I wanted to run after her and corner her at her door but I digressed.

I'll just give her some space to cool down. We've been dealing with a lot lately and Zo has been taking it all out on me.

We're supposed to show up to at my parents for dinner and it looks like I'm going to have to tell them about what's been going on.

*   *   *

"Hey baby," my mom stretched her arms out to embrace me.

"Hey mama."

"What's wrong?"

I sighed, "Zora had a miscarriage. We've been dealing with it privately but it's a lot to carry."

"I'm so sorry baby. How are you both doing?"

"Not good. Zora just ended things."

"She's just hurting baby. Losing a child changes a woman. How are you holding up?"

"I'm holding."

"Give Zora some time to come around. You both will be okay. Anyone that can handle your sisters is a keeper," my mom teased.

I smiled but inside my heart was shattered. Zora had evolved into my axis. Everything in my life revolved around that woman.

"I don't know if she will. I did something careless."

"What did you do son?"

"I told LaDana about the miscarriage."

"You did what? That lil' girl has been chasing behind you for years! You told her about your lady friend losing your child? Son you know better than that!"

I sat as if I was five year old child being scolded by mother. I was already beating myself up.

"I don't know what I was thinking mama."

"We all make mistakes son. Let her cool off and do what you can to make it right. If she really is done then you have to respect he decision and try to find peace."

"Yes ma'am."

"Hey, mama," my sisters bellowed coming through the front door. They showed up together which means they were out spending their husband's money up.

"Hey babies. I'm in here," she yelled back.

"Why you all up in here with your long face? What's wrong?"

I was silent. I didn't need them all in my business. Ever since Zo and my sister got into a fight they all somehow got cool. I was shocked because normally my sister holds grudges. I guess that made Zo official. She proved she can hold her own.

I loved that she wasn't fake or phony. Some people get close to your family to build leverage thinking it's going to help solidify their spot in the relationship.

"He and Zora broke up," my mom didn't hesitate to tell my business.

I cut my eyes at her but dared not mumble a word.

"What did you do?" Esdee asked.

"None of your business," I snapped.

"He told your lil' friend at the coffee shop that Zora had a miscarriage."

My mama had diarrhea at the mouth today for some reason. All of my business was just running out of her mouth.

"She was pregnant?"

"Yes Charlise," I didn't attempt to hide my irritation.

I hated when they got all in my business.

"Why would you tell LaDana about Zora's miscarriage? You know they can't stand each other. Do you know how devastating a miscarriage I for a woman?"

It was a shock hearing Esdee defend Zora. The two of them never got along. For her to say this means I really messed up.

"Soforhow do I fix it?"

"Give her time. It's the only thing you can do," Esdee said.

"If you love her I say you fight for her. Forget giving her time. That way when y'all make-up we can get started again on me a niece or nephew," she nudged me.

"Can we grieve the one we lost first!"

I grabbed my coat and headed home. I didn't have an appetite anyway.

I wondered what Zora was doing right now?

Would I look like a stalker if I drove by her apartment?

I didn't see her rental so I decided to go to the bookstore and do inventory. I refused to go home because it would only remind me that I was alone. No baby or woman. Just me again.

Confusion was an understatement when I saw Zora's rental parked in front of the store in her normal spot.

I couldn't get that car in park fast enough. I knew my baby would come to her senses and realize she overreacted.

I was livid when I walked in and caught Clayton embracing Zora.

"Get your hands off my woman! Are you out of your mind?" I yelled.

"Man, I was just telling her that I'm going to miss her being around here. It was really not that serious. You bugging dude. I'ma head out and let y'all talk," he huffed storming past me.

"Was that really necessary?" Zora asked.

"How was I supposed to act when every time I turn around he finding an excuse to be in your face?"

"Probably the same way you expected me when you always had your girlfriend from next door sniffing around every chance she gets. Look I didn't come here to argue with you. I just came to drop off your key," she stretched out her hand.

Her eyes never left mine. If she thought I was about to let those pretty brown eyes walk out of my life she really had no idea who Rohan Jefferson was.

I would fall back for now until I came up with a plan but I wasn't letting Zora go. Ever.

"If you want the car after it's repaired I will drop it off."

"Don't insult me. That was a gift. I told you whether we're together or not I'm going to do right by you.

ZORA

THREE WEEKS LATER

I guess Rohan was finally starting to get the picture. When we first broke up he would drive by my house every now and again. I saw his butt lurking in my neighborhood a few times. I pulled my white halter dress over my full boobs and admired myself in the mirror.

I was flawed but beautiful. There was the time I didn't see the beauty within myself so I allowed people who claimed to love me to mistreat me.

I spoke to Rohan one time to many concerning LaDana to the point I felt my feelings were being ignored.

Ding. Dong.

"Who is it?"

"You let that fine man go so who else is it going to be?" Sherica teased from the other side of the door.

"Girl, shut up and come in. I'm almost ready."

"Did you have to oil yourself in butter to get that white halter dress over all that booty and them hips," she laughed smacking my butt.

"Coconut oil," I laughed.

"Get your stuff and go so we can get in the club for free."

"Okay, let me put on my lip gloss and heels."

By the time we made it to the club it was jumping. People were littered throughout the parking lot smoking and drinking.

Sherica and I had started sipping on our Hennessy on the way to the club so we were feeling nice by the time we pulled up.

I wasn't looking for anything I just wanted to get out of the house. I was tired of thinking about Ro and my baby.

I just wanted to get out and let my hair down.

I haven't really talked to Jilly since the hospital. Seeing her with her daughter just reminded me that I was robbed of mine.

For the second time I was proven unworthy to be a mother. Even if it wasn't true that's how I felt inside.

I shook the thoughts of failure from my mind as I pushed my way through the crowd. I spoke with one of the hostess and told her we would pay to get into VIP.

She nodded and escorted us to the balcony that overlooked the club. The D.J. was mixing up some of the hottest joints out.

I watched as Sherica grinded on random dudes and enjoyed herself. Personally, I was ready to go. I was never cut out for the club scene.

Unfortunately, I rode with Sherica so I had to wait until she was ready.

"Nigga I told you I was going to see you," I heard an unfamiliar voice yell.

Pop!

Pop!

Pop!

Pop!

Some of us hit the floor while others ran for the one exit. I detested any establishment that had only one exit with all the random mass shootings.

With all the adrenaline pumping I barely noticed the sharp pain in my side. I must've landed on some glass or something.

I placed my hand over the spot where I felt the pain and felt something wet. I looked at my hand and it was covered in blood.

My hands trembled in fear as I felt my body slip into shock.

I was afraid to lift my head to see if Sherica was okay. I looked over at my clutch and pulled my phone out.

I dialed 9-1-1.

"Hello 911, what is your emergency?"

"I've been shot."

"What is your location ma'am?"

"I'm at club Ransom. I'm here with a friend but I don't know if she's okay. It's getting hard…to..breathe."

"I have an ambulance and police units on the way. Stay on the phone with me until they arrive."

"I can't," I told her ending the call.

I could feel my body getting weak and the adreline wearing off. I need to call Rohan. I needed him to know I love him.

I pressed his number from my recent call history. I waited on the other end hoping he would answer.

"Hello."

"I've been shot," I panted.

"What do you mean you've been shot? Where are you? I'm on my way!"

"Ransom."

"You know that place is a death trap! Stay on the phone with my baby. Please."

"I'll try."

I could feel myself now laying in a pool of blood. I could no longer feel my legs.

I tried everything within my power to cling to Rohan's voice.

"Zo! Zo!" I could hear him yell.

I just didn't have the wind in my lungs to respond.

His pleas were getting further and further away. The only thing I can think about at this moment is the last few weeks I've wasted being petty with a man I know was crazy about me.

If I had forgiven him and moved forward I would be here. Laying in my own blood that no longer felt warm but was cold as ice.

ROHAN

I zipped through traffic running all lights and anything that kept me from getting to my Zo. Those were not going to be the last words I heard from her. That woman was built for me and I should've fought for her harder.

She's always been worth the fight.

By the time I pulled up to the club it was utter mayhem. People were crying and screaming for their loved ones. Ambulance and police were lined up and down the street.

I went to each one looking for Zo.

"Sir, you need to get behind the line!"

"I'm looking for my wife!"

"Who is your wife?"

"Her name is Zora Mitchell!"

He got on his walkie-talkie and asked about Zora.

"Follow me sir. You almost missed her. Their own their way to the hospital. Did you want to follow them or ride with her?"

"I'm riding with her!"

When I climbed into the bus Zora was unconscious. They already had an IV in her and her white dress was stained all over with blood.

"Is she going to be okay?"

"It depends on the internal damage," the paramedic responded.

I held her tiny hands within mine and whispered in her ear, "You can't leave me. I'm marrying you woman!"

I was going to call both of our families once we made it to the hospital.

We exchanged contact information for each other's parents just in case situations like this occurred.

I would have my mother pick up Zora's mother on the way because I know she doesn't drive.

The trauma team was waiting on us when we arrived at the hospital.

They rushed Zora through some double doors.

"We're going to do everything we can to save her," she attempted to assure me before disappearing with the rest of her team.

My hand shook as I dialed my mother.

"Mama," I whimpered. "It's Zora. She's been shot."

"What? What happened? You know what never mind. Your father and I are on our way. I'll call your sisters."

"Mom, can pick up her mother? I'm about to call her so that she's ready when you get there."

"Absolutely baby. Anything you need."

I rambled off the address so my mom could write it down.

When I hung up I called Zora's mother. She freaked completely out.

I thought she was going to go into cardiac arrest. I told her my mom was on her way to give her a ride but she told me that Zora's father would bring.

I was a bit shocked because Zora told me how that all went down and it wasn't pretty.

I wonder if Zora knew her mom and dad were back in contact with one another.

I paced back and forth and prayed harder than I have in a long time. Begging God to spare the woman I love more than anything in this world.

I was miserable without Zora. The past three weeks I lost over twelve pounds.

I rarely went to the shop because it wasn't the same without her. I also couldn't stand the sight of LaDana.

I would never forgive her for the way she used what I confided in her to hurt Zora.

Looking back I understood now what I did wrong. I would spend my life making it up to her if she allowed me to.

"What happened?" Zora's mother cried.

"I don't know. She called me and told me she got shot. When I made it to where she was the paramedics had her ready to pull off. I jumped in and called you all once I made it. I'm still waiting for them to come back out and tell me something. There was so much blood I'm not sure where she got shot at."

"Ma'am! Ma'am! I need to know what's going on with my baby!" She slammed her fast on the counter repeatedly.

"Please calm down ma'am. As soon as the surgeon is done working on her, they will be out to tell you something. As of right now, she's in surgery. You will have to wait until she's out to find out more."

Reluctantly, Zora's mother stepped away from the counter.

The pressure of her daughter fighting for her life forced her knees to buckle. She hit the floor with such force I thought her fraile kneecaps would crumble beneath her.

Zora's dad went over to help her from the floor. When he sat her down he held her closely in his arms as if he was trying to protect her from the pain.

He couldn't hide his mask of distress either. I wondered if he and Zora had talked more.

If they hadn't he was definitely talking to her mama again.

As we all sat in the waiting room anxiously waiting to hear something, Jilly walked in.

"Oh my God, is she okay?"

Dry tears had worn through her make-up. The bags under her eyes bore witness that her new baby girl was keeping her up.

"We're still waiting. Zora has been in surgery for hours now."

"Does anyone know what happened?"

"No."

"I can probably fill y'all in," all of our eyes turned to Sherica.

I've only met her a few times when bringing Zora lunch to her job.

The dried blood on her milk chocolate complexion was evidence of her survival. Her white blouse was dirty as if she had crawled her on her elbow to survive the shoot out in the club.

"I was trying to get her out of the house because she's been down about the breakup. We just wanted to have a couple of drinks, let our hair down, and dance a little. I was on the dance floor, but Zo stayed in the VIP section. Right before they started shooting, I had to go to the bathroom. When the gunshots rang out, I ran to the door. I had to make sure Zo was okay. I didn't see her, so I thought maybe she got out of the building. I stayed in the bathroom until I heard the cops. I was getting questioned by the police; that's why I just now made it."

"I told her no new friends," Jilly rolled her eyes at Sherica.

"And you said that to say what?"

Sherica squared her shoulders, wanting all of the smoke from Jilly.

Jilly has always been this soft-spoken, laid back short-stacked woman.

Jilly pinched the bridge of her nose and exhaled.

"I know you're accustomed to making scenes in public places, but that's not how I operate. I'll see outside of these parameters."

"Nah, you can see me now, lil' mama," she gave a bitter laugh.

"Now is not the time for all this foolishness," Sabrina interjected.

Zora's dad, Sabian, sat quietly in the corner. He didn't really know any of us, so he was just observing.

"Is this the family of Zora Mitchell?"

The doctor favored a low budget Ellen in scrubs.

"Yes!" We all responded in unison.

"She came in with a gunshot wound to the abdomen. The bullet did ricochet and pierced her lungs causing them to collapse. There was some damage to her small intestines, so we had cut a few feet to repair the damage. Once we get her settled into a room, I want to warn you that she will have some tubes in her. She's going to have a nasogastric tube to remove fluid, air, and blood from her stomach. She also has an endotracheal tube to help her breathe. She lost a lot of blood, so we did have to give her a blood transfusion."

We all listened intently as she explained Zora's injuries.

Sabrina whimpered in Sabian's arms.

"When can we see her?" I asked.

"She's in observation right now. Once we make sure she's out of the woods entirely, we'll bring a couple of you back. Once she's in her room, you can take turns going in to see her. She will be in ICU until she can breathe on her own."

We exhaled a bit to find out at least she was still fighting. As promised, the doctor came back out to get Zora's mother and me.

I felt like a knife was plunged into my heart when I saw my baby lying there helpless.

Sabrina's throat thickened with sobs as she brushed Zora's hair from her face.

They had taken the time to clean her up. They had removed the blood-stained clothes from her shapely body. She no longer looked like she had been trampled under random people's feet.

I kissed her soft hands repeatedly.

"You got this baby," I whispered to her. "I'll never leave your side again," I promised her.

Over the next two weeks, those that loved Zora was in and out of her room.

I rarely left. If I wasn't with her, it was because I'd run out of clean clothes.

"What are you doing?" Sabrina asked coming into the room.

"The polish on her nails is starting to peel. She hates when her nails aren't done. I don't want her to wake up and seem them like this."

Sabrina smiled, "I just stopped by briefly before my meeting upstairs."

"Okay. Nothing has changed yet," I told Sabrina.

"It will. Zora's always been a strong child. She's an even stronger woman. Just trust God," she assured me.

"I am Sabrina. I know he's going to come through for her."

"Well, I'll be back after my appointment."

"Okay."

Once she was out of the room, I went back to painting Zora's nails.

While painting one of her nails, I noticed her hand lift.

Excitement raced through me. I stood to my feet to see my baby looking back at him.

I pressed the red bottom on her bed for the nurse.

"Yes, how can we help you?"

"She's woke! Can someone come in here and check on her?"

"Absolutely!"

A team of nurses and two doctors came into her room.

"Ms. Mitchell, your levels are exceptional. We're going to take your tube out."

Zora nodded her head.

They gave her a muscle relaxing medication to help her relax so that she would feel minor discomfort.

"Mr. Jefferson, she won't be able to talk because this tube she will have a severe sore throat. She won't be able to raise her voice if she's able to speak. She still may also be a bit short of breath as well," the doctor explained.

Zora was fortunate enough to have the same doctor who performed her surgery oversee her care the entire time she was in the hospital.

I waited anxiously for the tube to be pulled out. Zo was still loopy once it was, but she was one more step closer to bouncing back.

I've been carrying her five-carat diamond ring in my pocket since this happened.

I didn't care how long I had to wait for her to wake up. When that moment happened, I wanted to slip this ring on her finger.

I thought Sabrina would be back by now, but she may have gone home.

She's still been spending a lot of time with Sabian so she may be with him.

"Oh, my goodness! She's woke!" Sabrina said as she entered the room.

Just as I suspected, Sabian was right behind her.

Zora looked a bit puzzled to see them together.

I stepped back so they could be near her. I was just glad she was back.

"Can I speak to you both outside for a minute?"

They eyed each other but proceeded to follow me outside to the hallway.

"Sabian, I know you are just coming back into Zora's life but I wanted to ask for her hand in marriage. I know you don't really know me but I promise I spend my life making your daughter the happiest woman in the world."

He looked at Sabrina, "Well? You know him, I don't."

"I would be honored for Zora to have such a man by her side. He's been good to her since he's come into her life."

"Thank you Sabrina," I embraced her.

I knew Zora couldn't really speak but she could nod her head. That's the only confirmation that I needed if she agreed to make my life complete.

When we all walked back in a look of confusion was on Zora's face.

"What's wrong?" She mouthed.

"Oh, nothing sweety," Sabrina rubbed her head.

I walked over to her and pulled out the red box that was trimmed in gold.

I could see tears forming in her eyes.

I got down on one knee. Being tall was working in my favor at the moment. I was still able to see her face to face.

"Zora Mitchell, will you marry me?"

She grasped for me to come closer frantically shaking her head.

I slid the ring on her finger and wiped her tears. Fromt his day forward the only time this woman would shed cry during moments of happiness.

I have found the one whom my heart loves and I'm never letting her go.

ONE YEAR LATER.

"Push baby! You got this!" I coached Zo.

Two months after our honeymoon we found out she was pregnant. This time she decided to share her news with our family.

The overwhelming support from the beginning made such a huge impact on Zora.

All the positive energy, love and prayers ushered us into this moment.

Our baby boy was on his way.

Zora was so beautiful pregnant. I was nervous about her working but she said we wouldn't live in fear of what could be. She believed it only would caused what we feared most to manifest.

"You're doing great baby!" I continued to coach her.

"Get this boy out of me neeooowwwww!!" She screamed.

R.J. was scheduled to be delivered at a whopping nine pounds ten ounces.

We came up with R.J. because Zora insisted on him being a junior.

Zora insisted on bringing our son into this world without pain medicine. I was totally against it. I was all for her all natural holistic black woman vibe but pushing a ten pound baby out of your vagina was on another level.

Zora was set on doing things her way and I decided to support her.

This woman has amazed me with her resolve.

"Aaaaagggggghhh!!!!!"

Zora let out one last scream that produced our first born son.

Rohan Jefferson, II was absolutely perfect. The nurses rushed him off to clean him up.

They placed him on Zora's chest.

"We did it baby," she cried.

"You did it," I kissed her forhead.

I didn't think Zora could get any more beautiful but once again she proved me wrong. Seeing my son lying on her chest filled me with an overwhelming love and sense of completion.

I was filled with emotion. Everything that I thought I lost at one point in time has all been restored.

Zora was an unexpected blessing that I couldn't even imagine was possible for me to receive. As things unfolded between us our expectations of one another became a bit jaded. It's okay to have expectations of the one you love but you also have to calculate in space to allow them to grow.

Me and Zora have forced each other to evolve in unimaginable ways.

This woman has made me not only a husband but a father. I will love her until my last breath and even after then.

THE END